Flashbacks
(an unreliable memoir of the '60s)

By Morgan Smith

Flashbacks
(an unreliable memoir of the 60s)

Table of Contents

If You Remember the '60's...

Before I turned thirty, people I knew were telling me to write my memoirs. I thought this hysterically funny. I still do.

Now, though, I've hit that stage. You know. The one your parents hit around the time you graduated from college. The one where every single word anyone utters reminds them of when they were young. The one where they try to convince you that everything was better "back then".

Of course it was. Almost everything looks, tastes, smells and feels better at sixteen than at sixty.

Don't for one minute think I'm not conscious of the irony here.

****

Memory, as they say, is a damned elusive thing.

There are a whole lot of other adjectives you could slide in there: insubstantial, disconnected, misleading, slippery, those all come to mind, too. Especially, perhaps, when writing a memoir, where the attraction of attaching some kind of meaning to random events becomes almost overpowering.

Well, not "almost" – unavoidable would be more accurate. The need for humans to construct a narrative out of the scattered beads of life is the driving force behind everything from religion and philosophy to childcare and dress accessories, and memory can in no way be exempt.

Some things became apparent in the writing process, though.

It's not clear to me anymore which of the reminiscences I tell you here are wholly my own, are secondhand renderings of stories repeated as family lore, are incidents that have become compilations of different events which through repeated retellings have mashed together to form a single tale, or even, as science has proven happens to us all, are not even slightly my own memories, but have laid themselves down in me as if they were my very bones.

Still, I did not merely live through a period of enormous cultural change in the western world, but was an experiencing and participating member of the tribe.

It is a period that has become mythic, maligned and misunderstood.

When I watch the (always selective) film footage of those years and listen to the patronizing, clichéd and frequently ill-informed commentary that inevitably accompanies it, or when I read academic studies claiming as hard and as immutable a divide between "Flower Power" and "the New Left" as the Great Wall of China (to the point where the writer seems sure that the two groups never shopped in the same supermarkets, let alone talked, supported and engaged with each other in protest rallies and at parties), I have a hard time believing that these are the same times and events I was a part of.

I am struck by how intensely difficult it is to convey the raw reality of those days; how impossible it is to communicate the feeling of that time – the ineradicable, blatant, exuberant and encompassing joy of it.

The gulf between the experience and the interpretation appeared immediately, and grew exponentially. As early as the late '70s, people becoming parents were whitewashing their own past, repudiating it, revising it, even erasing it in many cases, and the tendency only got worse. Meanwhile, people who had not been old enough, or had not lived in places or come from families that allowed the experience were becoming curious.

What, exactly, had been going on out there?

****

More than that, though, I feel as though the world – at least the western/North American world – needs to be reminded of this time. Of a time when we were not passive. When we had hope and belief, and acted on it. When we understood that to change ourselves was to change the world.

So, here I am, sorting through my brain and trying to grasp onto that past, and making an attempt to communicate what it all felt like, still feels like, to me. In the end, these recollections are a revelation to me as well: it becomes difficult to separate those things that might have been universally and viscerally true from those that were unique to me.

It isn't, therefore, *the* memoir of the sixties – it's merely mine.

And being mine, I am now aware that the arc of my life in those years followed the arc of the era's own events.

Something special, something shared: that was real. It did happen. It grew out of the decade that preceded it and extended itself into the one that followed, and it's plain that the effects are still being felt, even if only in the form of a backlash – and because of that, it is not a trivial thing. It is worth being remembered and not something to be carelessly discarded.

It shaped the world and it was incredible.

If I can come near to communicating something about that, does it matter if I remember being at a demonstration in 1966 that actually occurred a year later? Will it change the internal, emotional truth if someone else's life event is somehow entangled into mine? I don't think I have done that – I am as sure as I can be that these things are my own experiences – but as noted above, science says that I *will* feel and *will* believe this, all evidence to the contrary.

Thus my subtitle – an admittedly vain attempt to head off an avalanche of emails and PMs and Facebook posts, telling me that nothing I remember can be believed if I didn't get this one detail or that one chronology right.

One other disclaimer: most of the names of the people involved have been altered or changed outright. All of them had at the time or went on to have both public and private lives that are their own affair. Some of them are dead. In any and all of these cases, I feel that it would be churlish and unfair to reveal aspects of their lives that they might not wish exposed. If they wish to claim themselves – well, that's up to them, not me.

And one dedication: when you come to the end, you might feel I should have dedicated this to my parents. But, no. For them, the book itself, and the life I've managed so haphazardly to live is that dedication.

Instead, I'd like to offer this up to someone I have never met: Jackson Browne, who made the words and music that marched beside me, in all the years that have come after. If anyone has managed to encapsulate my life experiences for me, it's been that guy. Thank you.

1959

It's spring, and we're going to New York.

I'm not really that interested in New York. I am not even really sure what New York is, but I don't really care.

What I am interested in is that I am going to ride on a *train*!

I love trains. I've seen them on television and in picture books, and I want more than anything in the world to ride on one. I watch Captain Kangaroo every morning. I draw them on the backs of the scrap paper my dad brings me from work. I play trains at home, dragging chairs from the dining room and the kitchen, arranging them in lines, filling them with stuffed animals and dolls, and making train noises. Trains are the most wonderful, exciting things I know of in my universe.

If a four-year-old can be said to have an ambition, mine is to ride on a train.

My mother tells me that I have, in fact, already taken train journeys, when I was very, very small, but I only partway believe her. My mother is utterly trustworthy, and I know that babies do nothing but sleep, eat and get burped, but still. How on earth could I forget being on a train?

Union Station is enormous and echo-ey and mostly marble, with hard, long benches. We acquire an elderly man with a sort of pushcart who takes charge of the luggage, and he and I have an intensely interesting discussion about how lucky he is to spend all day at the train station. He compliments me on my spring coat, but inside my head I make a 'messy face' because I don't really like my coat. It is made of some scratchy, nubbly black and white fabric, and its only real advantage is that the buttons are very large, so I can do them up by myself.

My father stops at a kiosk and lets me pick out a chocolate bar to share later. On the *train*! I am trying very hard not to jump around and scream for pure pleasure, because I have promised to be on my very best behaviour, but it's getting more difficult as we head towards the platform.

My father understands, I think, because he suggests we walk down to the end together and see the caboose. I can't help myself, I am doing little hoppy-skippy steps as we go, but he doesn't tell me to stop, we just weave our way down through the knots of other people waiting to get on the train.

The caboose is much bigger than I expect, and the red is not as bright, but it is still exciting. In combination with the oily smells and the hugeness of the space and the crowds, I feel as though something quite momentous is about to happen. As we walk back, my dad is explaining about dining cars and sleeping berths, which we won't have because New York is not really that far. Sleeping berths are for when you go on train trips that take days and days, he says. Although I will have to sleep on the train, because we won't get to New York until tomorrow, only I won't be in a sleeping berth.

Now, he says, we can go look at the engine. We wave at my mother as we go by, and she waves back, but we don't stop till we get to the engine. There are men in greasy overalls and rags stuffed in their back pockets, getting in and out of the engine and shouting.

There are also some other kids, with their parents. They are mostly boys. We smile shyly at each other and watch the men working on the train. The dads light cigarettes and grin at each other and at us, all wide-eyed and amazed at how big and almost scary the engine is.

"Kids." they murmur to each other.

Except this one dad, who scowls and says "Trains, fer crissake. I blame the goddam schools."

I am a little shocked. Not because of the 'bad words'. I'm not allowed to say 'bad words' (except if I am by myself) and my parents try hard not to use any around me, all of the grownups I know try not to, but I hear them all the same. I know what 'bad words' are, I have to, or how else could I avoid using them? But he sounds so angry, and I cannot understand how anyone could be angry in such a magnificent place, surrounded by these wonderful trains and obviously about to actually get to ride on them. How can you not love trains?

My father takes my hand and says that we should go back, since they are now calling out that the train is ready for boarding. When we get back to where my mother has been waiting, we find that she has already managed the stowing of the luggage, with help from the man with the pushcart as well as two other men who feel she must be too frail to manage suitcases by herself.

We say goodbye to the pushcart man. I say thank you, very politely, because that's what you do when people do nice things for you. My father gives him something, and he goes off, whistling.

The seats we have on the train are arranged like a breakfast nook around a fold-up table. The cloth on them is dark red plush, rather stiff and bristly, and the windows are huge.

I don't ask to sit beside the window. I know this is part of 'being good' – not asking for things. Grownups are allowed to, but not children. When children ask, it is being bratty, and bratty children are not appreciated. But my parents seem aware of my longing and I get the seat with the window facing the same way the train will be going and I will be able to see Everything!

Out the window I can see other trains, and more men in overalls, and I can ignore all the grownups jostling around in the space between the seats and the talking, which seems very loud. Eventually, though, everyone is settled in and it gets very quiet, a bit like church, where everyone is waiting for something important to start, and I completely understand this, because I feel the same way.

There's noise, and squealing sounds and rumbles, and the train very slowly begins to move.

****

The conductor is coming around.

My father has spread out his work on the fold-up table. He's grading first-year papers, I think, because in addition to the stack of papers, he has gotten out a red pencil. Only first and second year papers get red pencil. After that, it is blue, except very occasionally, and by dint of listening carefully to my parents' discussions I have figured out that a third year paper that gets red pencil is a very bad thing.

Every so often, he stops and reads something aloud to my mother, and both of them laugh.

Now that the initial excitement of movement has subsided, and I have watched the telephone poles and the backs of factory buildings whizz by for several minutes, and had a discussion with my father about speed and counting the seconds between one telephone pole and another – a discussion I do not actually comprehend but feel may be quite important – I have decided to stand on my seat and examine the interior of the train.

My mother makes me take my shoes off before I do this, but despite the fact that I am never allowed to stand on seats at home, she doesn't seem to feel that the rule applies here. So I see exactly when the conductor enters our car, and I watch him as he looks over every ticket, and then punches a tiny, exact hole on it, and moves on.

I tell my father he will need to have the tickets out and ready. He seems glad that I am keeping track and looking out for us, and produces the tickets. My mother is reading but she looks up from her book and smiles at me.

The conductor is from Quebec. He speaks French to us, and my mother and he exchange information on where they are from. He asks me how old I am and seems amazed that I am four.

He lets me punch our tickets. My father helps, holding my hands over the puncher and giving that extra push down so it punches a neat little square just where it ought to. I am now so overwhelmed with joy that I can barely say 'Merci', and it is several minutes before I feel capable of speech again.

When I get restless, my father takes me to between the cars, where it is almost outdoors and you can really feel the train rumbling and clacking under your feet, and it is quite hard to stand still because the train sways and rattles. If I stand on my tiptoes, I can look out and see the world rushing past, and the wind blows wisps of hair out from my braids.

There's not much to do on the train besides look and listen. Although my English is not quite as good as my French, I still understand quite a lot but some words are hard, and I always ask about them, because my father says understanding is important. People are talking a lot, and not always quietly, and they say things that are apparently grownup jokes because then they laugh, very loud, as if they were at home. It's puzzling, because my parents have taught me to be quieter when you go out to restaurants or church. Trains must be different.

"Daddy, what are beatniks?"

"Oh," he says, "Beatniks live under the tables in cafes in Greenwich Village."

"And," says my mother, who has put away her book and is now doling out sandwiches she brought with us for the trip, "They say 'Cool, daddy-o' and snap their fingers instead of clapping."

I giggle, but I like this. Between bites of cheese sandwich, I try to snap my fingers. It is harder than it looks.

After sandwiches, my mother agrees to read to me. She has brought 'Le Petit Prince' which is my favourite. I use my folded-up coat as a pillow and lie down with my head in her lap, and listen to her voice. She likes reading aloud, and makes all the voices sound different, and even the describing parts are exciting. When we get to the part about the king, though, I sit up, and my father puts down the red pencil, and we act out the yawning part for her. My father shakes his finger at me and wiggles his eyebrows furiously, making us laugh.

At some point, I must have fallen asleep, because when I

open my eyes, it is night-time, and the allure of the windows is lost. My mother has moved to the other side to sit with my father, who has his arms around her, and they are dozing. One of them has tucked my father's coat around me, and I snuggle down, breathing in the smell of tobacco and home, and drift off again.

****

In New York, the station is filled with people and very noisy, and I am a little frightened, because we are supposed to meet our friends, Sam and Jackie, and I don't see how we can find them in this crowd. But we do find them, and Jackie hugs me and asks how I am, but then she is hugging my mother and asking how she is, and I don't get a chance to answer.

Sam and Jackie have a car because they live in Philadelphia and don't get to ride the train to New York. The car is far away, but Sam picks me up and carries me, because I am "short stuff" and will get tired. I disagree – I can walk quite far – but Sam is nice, and tells me silly jokes, so I don't mind.

We are staying at a hotel. It is called the Statler-Hilton, and Jackie laughs when she is telling my parents why we all can afford to stay there: it is having something called renovations, and so most of the rooms are not usable. But the fun part is that because they are working on the electricity, everything you touch gives you a little shock.

"It's the 'Static-Hilton'," Sam says.

They are right – whenever you touch anything not made of wood or plastic, a tiny zap nips out at you. All of us spend a lot of time running around the two hotel rooms, testing what is shocky and what is not. It's very exciting.

We have lunch at the hotel. It's a restaurant: there are white tablecloths and silverware that has heavy handles. The waiters don't talk directly to me. They keep looking at my dad when I say what I want to eat. I think maybe my English is not the same as theirs, because it is true that I have to listen very hard to understand them. Some of their words come out differently from the way people say them at home.

I have Clam Chowder. I want the Manhattan kind, because I have never heard of it before, and that's the kind my father orders, but he says it is not at all like the kind I am used to, and suggests I would be happier with the kind called 'New England'. We make a deal that I can have a taste of his, and if I like his better he will swap with me.

Swap is a new word for me. It has a good sound, and I murmur it under my breath several times, to fix it in my mind.

My father is right, though. His chowder is tomato-ey and thin, and hardly tastes like clams at all. Mine is nicer, and the waiter brings me extra crackers, too.

At night we go to a restaurant called The Bamboo Hut. The waitresses are very tall ladies dressed in brightly-coloured dresses with trailing sleeves that my mother says are called 'kimonos'. There are little rooms around the outside part of the restaurant which have sliding doors. When they open the doors to bring food in, I can see people kneeling on the floor around low tables.

I am disappointed that we won't get to kneel on the floor, but have to sit at an ordinary table. My father says it would probably get uncomfortable, but I think from the sound of his voice that he is secretly a little disappointed, too.

The kimono-ladies have very complicated hairstyles, held up by beautiful hair ornaments with complicated, twisted-wood patterns and tiny bits of faceted metal hanging from the wood, and they catch the light in little sparks. I am fascinated by this, but alarmed when Jackie asks if I would like to do my hair like that, too, because she knows where the ornaments come from.

I give my mother a panicky look, because the hairstyles look uncomfortable, like the way it feels with barrettes. My mother and I have agreed on no more barrettes, because we are united in the understanding of how they hurt your head.

She just laughs and says "Jackie, it's hard enough doing her braids in the morning," and that's that.

On the way back to the hotel, my father promises me I can have another installment of the ongoing story he is telling me. I love my father's stories in the same way I love my mother reading books to me: his voice is like magic, and I can close my eyes and see all the things he describes.

Sam asks what the story is. When he hears that it is
called 'The Iliad', he stops and looks at me, skipping
backwards out of the store where we stopped to buy
bottles of wine and he says,

"You know that kid's gonna to be a holy terror someday,
don't you?"

"I certainly hope so," my father says.

****

My mother tells me, in later years, that we went to the
Museum of Modern Art the next morning. If we did, it
made no impression on me, and I remember nothing
about it. What I do remember is walking along the
pavement singing 'Sur Le Pont d'Avignon' quietly to
myself, and looking into the windows of something that
is not quite a cafeteria or a sitting-down restaurant, but
still has food and is called an 'Automat'; and I remember
eating soft pretzels with mustard on them for lunch.

After that, my mother, Jackie and I go to a very big
department store for The Sales. Before we can go in, I
have to promise to stay very close to either Jackie or my
mother, because at ChristmassanNewYears I got lost at
Eaton's, in the ladies' department. It was very upsetting,
I got quite scared, and I cried at the cashier's desk till my
mother came and found me.

I don't argue, I just promise. From my side, it seems

unfair, because I did not, in fact, wander off – it was my mother, in my view, who disappeared. But she is still a little cross about it, so I say that I will be extra-good about this.

She buys me a new spring coat. It's blue, which is one of my favourite colours, and it has a velvet collar. The buttons are not too small, and they have tiny pretend diamonds on them, which I am very impressed by.

But in the evening, it gets really exciting. We are going out, not just to dinner, but to cafes, which I remember is where the beatniks are.

My mother has made me a surprise, an outfit that is just like hers and Jackie's. I have a black skirt, and a black knitted sweater to wear over my white blouse, and even a little black beret – these feel very grown up, and I get to wear my hair loose and out of my braids, just like my mother. We pose, all three of us, for pictures by my father and Sam. Jackie has blonde hair, which shows up really well against her black sweater, but I think my mother is prettiest of all.

We go to a gypsy restaurant. My mother has borscht, which is beet soup, and a plate of dumplings with a sort of gravy over them. She shares the borscht with me, because I love beets, and I have a salad with Russian dressing and some tastes of my father's bowl of a spicy stew. I am not a picky eater. I am not allowed to be. I have to taste everything on my plate, even when I know I don't like something, because 'Tastes Change'. But I am not very interested in food, and I don't understand how you can spend so much time eating it.

The restaurant has a man with a violin and a big lady who sings. They go around to every table and sing right at you, in a language I don't understand. When they come to us, I like it, but suddenly I realize that there are tears running down my face and I don't know, exactly, why. I squish down in my chair and push my face into my mother's arm beside me, upset and embarrassed: this is not 'good manners' for restaurants.

But no one is angry. Maybe I don't know why I am crying, but everyone else seems to. My mother strokes my hair, and the man with the violin and the lady singer make sighing sounds and say "There, there" and pat my arms, as if I have done something good, not stupid.

After that we go to the cafe. It's dim and smoky and pretty crowded, but even while we are standing just inside the door getting used to the light, people are calling out my parents' names, and Sam and Jackie's names. They rearrange chairs for us, and I guess that cafes are like grown up parties, except with tables and waitresses like in restaurants. The talk is all the same: music and books and Civil Rights, which is making sure everyone is treated nicely, and are allowed to go to school. I don't go to school, but my mother says I will, soon.

I look under the table. No one is there. My father sees me doing this and encourages me to look harder, so after a while, since no one objects, I move out, looking carefully under more tables. I ask around, but no one has seen any beatniks.

But it's nice here. Unlike restaurants, I am free to wander, and everyone seems friendly. Ladies let me sit in their laps, admire my beret and give me sips of cappuccino, impressed that I don't make faces. I like coffee drinks, although at home mine are more milky-ey and less coffee-ey. Everyone asks my age, and, like the train conductor, seem amazed that I am four already. They ask me to describe the beatniks, so they can let me know if they see any, and when I explain about the finger-snapping I have to show them, although I still haven't figured out how to make the right noise happen. When I say "Cool, daddy-o", they laugh, a lot.

I ask about the drawing that one man is doing in a big sketchbook, and he lets me see, and then he lets me have a page out of the book and lends me a pencil, so that I can draw him a picture. It's a picture of my friends at home, playing on the swings, and he likes it, he says, because I have put fingers and toes on everyone. I had to count, very carefully, under my breath, to make sure all of them are fives. People only ever have fives.

Back at my table, I have hot chocolate, with some of my mother's coffee poured in. There are more chairs squished in, as more people want to talk to us, and one of them is Ellis.

Ellis is someone I know, because he came to visit us just after ChristmassanNewYears, and he plays the banjo. Disappointingly, he has no banjo tonight. He's talking to my dad about something called a visa, but he stops to say hello to me and ask me about my dog, Lapin. Lapin is pink and was made by a friend of my grandmére's. Lapin is my constant companion and when it is bath day for Lapin, my mother says I am sad and lonely and cannot be appeased with chocolate. When he came to visit us, Ellis was confused as to why a dog would be called 'Rabbit', and I had to explain that pink things are rabbit things. He has gotten over this confusion now and only asks if Lapin stayed at home.

"He stayed at the hotel," I explain. "Daddy says Lapin doesn't like crowds, and might get lost."

We go out into the night, and to another cafe. There are no beatniks under tables here, either, but Ellis does magic tricks for me with a nickel I find on the floor, and an older lady gives me a caramel and shows me how her amber beads can make a napkin stick to it.

It goes on very late. There is some poetry, and then some music, all very casual, and the people who have played already are asking my dad and Ellis if they will play too. They get up and borrow guitars and sing 'Tom Dooley' and 'Good Night Irene' which I know from listening to records at home.

Then we go back to the hotel. There are more of us than we started with, and so the car is very crowded and I sit on my father's lap in the front seat.

When we get to the hotel, the doorman says, "I can see someone who's on her way to bed!"

"Yeah, who?" my father asks and we all go down some stairs, leaving the doorman to be scandalized, to a place that is decorated with pretend palm trees and coloured lights. We get plastic flower necklaces called 'leis' and the drinks are served in coconut shells and in hollowed out pineapples. On the stage, there is first a man telling jokes that I don't understand, and then a line of ladies wearing shimmery grass skirts and dancing what is called a "hula".

After that, there is a band and dancing, and once the drinks have come (mine has a lot of fruit in it as well as being served inside a fruit, which is interesting) we take turns getting up to dance. I dance with Sam, who lets me stand on his shoes, and with both my parents, who are good about whirling me around and doing what are called "dips". When they dance just as the two of them, they seem perfectly matched, doing everything together, even when they are not looking at each other. I like watching them do this, and I notice other people like to watch them as well. Even other dancers make a little extra space for them.

At some point it is just the five of us, and we are back in the hotel room. I have my pajamas on, and suddenly, Sam and my father burst out of the bathroom, clad only in bath towel skirts and the leis, and they dance around the room, doing the hula. At the end they give me all the plastic leis, and we all fall on the bed, laughing, while Jackie makes drinks.

****

The next day is quieter. We go to a place called "Cloisters", which seems mostly like a park, where my father takes pictures of my mother. She is wearing her "Garbo" look: she has borrowed a pair of my father's trousers, and a tie, and has a soft silky blouse on. I don't what "Garbo" means but my mother looks beautiful and exotic and mysterious. I have my new coat on, and Sam and Jackie play hide-and-seek with me. Sam is pretty big and does not hide very well.

My father asks me how I feel about lunch, and I breathe "Automat?" hopefully. He makes a face, and Sam laughs, but everyone agrees that we can, just this once, go to one.

The Automat is odd and exciting, although the food is not very nice, really. There is too much butter on the bread of my sandwich, and the fruit salad is boring, but the excitement of choosing food displayed in tiny glass boxes, and putting coins in to get your choices, that part is enough fun for me to make eating worthwhile.

At this point, the understanding that this trip will have two train journeys is a kind of revelation for me. My parents seem tired and subdued, but I have enough energy for all of us, and make myself useful by pointing out all the interesting things around.

The conductor on this train is not at all friendly, which is sad. I think he would be happier at some other job, since the joy of train travel seems to be lost on him, but I don't tell him that. On the other hand, for some reason, we get to see much more of the train this time. First there is the bar car, where I have what is called a Shirley Temple and the bartender gives me my own bowl of peanuts. Later on, instead of sandwiches, we do, in fact, go to the dining car, where I share with my father a beef bourguignon that is not anywhere as good as when my mother makes it.

****

There might well be some important, life-changing meaning to this. Certainly, it is an experience few people of my age can lay claim to.

But frankly, what I remember most is the trains.

In our kitchen, I stand on a chair, stirring an enormous vat of chili as my mother and I intone:

> *"Eye of newt, and toe of frog,*
> *Wool of bat, and tongue of dog,*
> *Adder's fork, and blind-worm's sting,*
> *Lizard's leg, and owlet's wing..."*

All the adults laugh at us, and then chant "Double, double toil and trouble; Fire burn, and cauldron bubble." right on cue.

I like making them laugh and Shakespeare is good for this. When I am six and enter a room to ask "What fresh hell is this?" everyone laughs. When sent to wash my hands, I murmur "Out, damned spot!", and everyone laughs.

But when I remark at a funeral of a rather unbeloved cousin twice removed that it's a "consequence devoutly to be wished" - there is a shocked silence.

Quotations are tricky.

A Drum Major for the Cause (Part 1)

Like all my friends, I start school with excitement and impossible dreams. School, I believe, is a grownup place, where the mysteries of the adult world will unfold. Despite various older children filling us with dread about sitting still for hours, Not Answering Back, and something ominous called "The Strap", I assume it will be wonderful because my parents say it will be. They have looked hard for a school that I will like, and I go with my mother on a special shopping trip to buy School Clothes and the mysterious School Supplies, which turns out to be crayons.

****

There are ten of us in our class and we all mostly know each other, because our parents are friends, so our games and conversations are pretty ordinary extensions of what we would do on our own. We are introduced to things like Chalkboards, Milk-and-Cookies, Show-and-Tell, and Naptime, which I find stupid and boring because I haven't had to have Naptime since I was a baby.

Over the summer, I have discovered how to read. Reading seems to be the thing that separates grownups from children, and by applying the concepts of the alphabet letters having sounds of their own and matching those sounds to the letters in books, I have worked out the code. It is a pretty momentous day: I march downstairs to my mother, book in hand, to announce my accomplishment. She at first seems sceptical, thinking I am merely working from memory of books that have already been read to me. I offer a demonstration by sounding out the headline on the newspaper she'd been reading over coffee.

When my father comes home, and I demonstrate it for him, we get to go to down to the corner store for ice cream to celebrate with. After that, I wake each morning anticipating the metamorphosis into grownuphood, convinced that this is something that can be accomplished overnight[1]. After a week or two, it occurs to me that there might be more to it. I decide that school will probably be the answer.

Once in the classroom, however, it becomes clear that we will not be learning very much, at least not right away. Not everyone can say the whole alphabet, for a start, or recognize all the numbers, so we embark on mastering this as a group. This is fine with me. Each day, we draw a letter on huge pieces of paper, and then draw things that begin with that letter, and although the reading part has come easily for me, drawing the letters is new.

Teacher seems nice enough, but some of her behaviour is not what I have been taught is right. She is not fair, and her unfairness is directed only at one of us, my friend Larry.

---

[1] A misconception possibly reinforced by adults constantly insisting that a good night's sleep would "help me grow up big and strong".

Larry's mom does Civil Rights and Peace with my mother, so Larry and I have played together with my friends Molly and Shosh outside when our mothers are at meetings at Mrs. Lipschitz' house. Marjorie I don't know as well, but we met when our mothers took us to Open Day at the ballet school, and we will be in the same ballet class next year. In fact, the only person we are not already all friends with is Bobby, who is new to Toronto. He only knows one person, which is Larry, because their fathers work at the same hospital. So Bobby and Larry are friends.

Bobby is different from most of us. He is bigger than the rest of us, he has more confidence than most four- or five-year olds do, and he has a naturally rebellious and anti-authority spirit. It is Bobby who decides what games we will play, and how we will play them, and we let him, mostly, because otherwise, he can be difficult.

Even more daringly, he does not always listen to Teacher. He plays just that minute longer after she says Playtime is over, and at Naptime he frequently gets up and wanders over to play with a truck instead, pointedly showing that Teacher is not in charge of him, without quite going over into some indefinable territory of actual disobedience.

But Teacher ignores this, anyway. She is focused on Larry.

She jeers at Larry's last name, which I know you should never do, because names are not your own choice. She makes fun of his letters when he draws them, although they look no more spindly and awkward than everyone else's letters. She snaps questions out at him in a terrifying voice, so that Larry, a naturally shy boy anyway, can only whisper his answers, giving her the opportunity to say "Speak Up!" in a nasty tone. And, although we are supposed to be learning to line up alphabetically by last name, she makes him stand at the end of the line, even though, according to the letters, he should be beside Shosh, who is an "H".

It starts with the littlest things first, but each day seemed to bring a new form of rudeness. By the end of the second week, we are all aware that something is very, very wrong, and when we are out on the playground waiting for our mothers to pick us up, we talk about Teacher. Talking behind someone's back is not nice, we know that, but we are worried, because she is a grownup, and she is Teacher, and she is doing everything our parents have taught us is wrong to do. Molly says, greatly daring, that she does not like Teacher at all.

"Awww, she's just an old bat," says Bobby. "I'd like to punch her in the nose."

Around the third week, Teacher seems to think that we need to treat Larry the same way she does. We are frightened, and we don't want to. The playground conversations become very difficult. Andy says we are supposed to do what Teacher wants – it's the Rules. We could get in trouble. Trouble with Teacher means being sent to the corner.

I am not in favour of being rude to Larry, even if it

means getting sent to the corner. The general nature of dinner-table conversation about Civil Rights drifts through my mind. I say that if we all refuse to do what Teacher wants, on this one thing, I don't think we will be punished.

"She'll send us to the corner," Andy repeats this twice, in tones of dread.

"She couldn't. Not if all of us together don't do what she wants."

"Why not?" Marjorie asks.

"Because," I say, triumphantly, "there aren't enough corners!"

Bobby agrees. He brags that if she sends him to the corner, he just won't go.

"You'll get The Strap," says Andy. He has older sisters, so he is our source on this, although no one has explained in precise terms what 'The Strap' really is.

It all comes to a head on the day we learn to draw the letter 'J'.

****

Despite regular Sunday rituals of church and dinner at my grandparents' house, I am not really aware of what religion is. My father says sitting quietly in church is good training, although he does not say for what. Since it is not discussed much, I have not given serious thought to what is said or done there, other than insisting on a seat in the middle and not near the aisles, where the incense makes it hard to breathe.

But I am aware that people go to different churches on Sundays, and that in Shosh's family, they don't go at all. I am envious, because her parents take her to the park on Sundays, instead.

Teacher asks us to name things that begin with 'J'. This turns out to be quite hard. We manage to come up with things like 'jumping jacks' and 'jalopy', which Bobby says is a lousy car his father won't pay six bucks for. Teacher says 'jalopy' and 'bucks' are slang, which is not allowed in school. When she turns her back, he makes a face at her.

Then she looks at Larry and says, "You're a 'J', aren't you, Larry? You're a 'J' because 'J' is for 'Jew-boy'."

All of a sudden, I feel as if I can't breathe properly. Because I know there's a word for this, and it's a very bad one, one that grownups lower their voices for. It has to do with Civil Rights, but also to do with something called The War, and that some kind of line, a line I had never before known to exist in the real world, has been crossed.

"So – Jew-boy – can you tell me something that begins with a 'J'? Speak up, I can't hear you when you mumble. No? Nothing?"

There are two big, round tables in our classroom, but up till now we have only used the one, because although it is only meant for eight, Teacher likes to keep us all together. Now, since Larry is silent, not offering any 'J' words, she tells him to take his paper and his crayons over to the other table.

And something in me just shatters. I watch Larry, very near tears, pick up his things and move over, and I can't stand it. I get up, grab my paper and crayons and follow him.

Teacher announces, in a very angry voice, that I am a Jew-lover. Are there any other Jew-lovers here? She wants to know.

This turns out to be a mistake. Shosh picks up her things and walks deliberately over to join us, and then Bobby stands up and says loudly that he thinks the other table looks more comfy. Marjorie, who has a not-very-secret crush on Bobby, immediately follows him, and within a very few seconds, eight of us are at the other table. Larry still looks as if he will cry, so I offer my crayons to share. I am the only one with the extra-large box and so everyone likes to borrow the exotic colours it has. Only Andy and Tommy are still at the first table, but this may be only because Teacher is standing between them and us, and she is really, really angry.

She talks non-stop, her voice getting louder and louder. Her face is red and blotchy, and we don't understand even a quarter of what she is saying, it is just a stream of horrible words with her face all twisted up.

We do what kindergarteners everywhere do when grownups scare them with this much anger. We burst into tears, wailing in utter terror at this complete loss of stability in our world. This makes Teacher get even louder, and use more words that we know, instinctively, are bad ones.

Suddenly there are other grownups in the room. Teacher is still yelling for the first little bit, but then she stops, practically mid-sentence. The other teachers who have come in are staring at her, aghast, because they have heard those terrible, terrible words and her angry voice, and they've seen her red and twisted angry face.

Somehow, they calm things down. Teacher is gone now, and the other teachers dry our tears with hastily produced handkerchiefs and Kleenex tissues, and get us to blow our noses. We are shepherded next door into the other kindergarten room to have another round of Milk-and-Cookies, and a story while we lie on Naptime mats until our mothers arrive and one by one, they take us home.

I don't go to school the next day. Instead Mrs. Lipschitz brings Larry over, and Mrs. Fields and Mrs. Hebert come too, and Molly and Shosh and Larry and I go up to my playroom and haul out my collection of Matchbox cars to play with, making hills to drive on by wrinkling up the area rugs. Downstairs, our mothers talk grownup things. At one point, we hear them laughing, very loud, and Mrs. Hebert saying, "Jeez, did they even talk to her before she was hired?" but then their voices sink down low again.

When it comes time for Larry to go home, Mrs. Lipschitz hugs me very hard, and says I'm a great kid.

Later, when my mother has set me up with her at the kitchen table to help make salad, she tells me first that she is proud of me. She emphasizes that I did the right thing by not listening to Teacher and standing up for Justice, even if, normally, disobeying Teacher would be wrong. She explains how I was right to know that this time was different. But then she asks me, if things were so bad, why it was I didn't talk to her about it?

"You should always tell Mummy these things," she says.

I have no explanation. I can't find any words for her. I concentrate on ripping up lettuce into bite-sized pieces as if my life depends on it, because I am having a terrible time figuring any of this out. I have assumed, up till this moment, that when my parents send me to school or anyplace else, that they somehow still know everything that will go on there.

Even at this point, I am still puzzling out if she truly means she did not know what Teacher was doing and saying, every minute that I was there. That there could be things my parents do not know is not something I am able to take in.

****

We had a new Teacher after this, much younger and

prettier, who still taught us how to draw letters in much the same way, but was better at reading stories and adamantly played no favourites. Aware, I think, that this was what would later be called 'a teachable moment', she emphasized Fair Play, Tolerance and Equality at every point possible, and managed to corral even Bobby's incipient anarchy into something positive and useful by putting him in charge of tidying up the toys before Naptime.

My grandmére likes two things about Toronto: the ballet, and the restaurant in Eaton's department store. So, every spring when they come to visit, she convinces me into a party dress and my black patent leather maryjanes, and we go to see whatever matinee that the National Ballet is doing, and then afterwards, we meet my grandpére at the restaurant. They like to have what they call "high tea"[2], which means a lot of tiny, crustless sandwiches and cream-filled pastries, washed down with china cups of very sweet, milky tea.

Meanwhile, my grandpére, who has spent our ballet-watching time at secondhand bookstores, shows us what he has bought, quizzes me about what I like to read, and then sorts among his purchases for the book he picked out specially for me. It is always leather-bound and dusty, and because he is fascinated both by Britain and the theatre, his gifts give no real thought to my age.

---

[2] It wasn't until I went to live in England, many years later, that I discovered how wrong this terminology was.

By the time I am ten, I have worked my way through Oscar Wilde, Bernard Shaw and Henrik Ibsen, and am starting in on Clifford Odets and Noel Coward.

Learning Curve

I know, looking back, that the first decade of my life feels like a kind of gift. I can see it from this distance as if it were a placid lake I sailed on, unruffled by winds or storms.

But this is an image of the whole of it and not the day-to-day as it was lived.

****

I am seven, and I am being bullied at school.

It isn't constant, and it is not as if I am an outcast. I've got a whole classfull of friends. My teacher sends home reports that I am reasonably attentive, well-behaved and good at my schoolwork.

But for Mandy, I am some kind of challenging signpost – the red satin cape to her angry toro.

I honestly don't know what I have done to become her target. The first time I laid eyes on her was a micro-second before she quite purposefully knocked me down in the hallway outside of my classroom.

Something about me offends her, although she has never seen me before this, and from then on, every few days, Mandy rounds up a couple of classmates and terrorizes me all over the playground.

She is a year ahead of me, and big for her age anyway,

and I am not – I am the class shrimp, to be honest. In school pictures, I am always in the centre of the front row, looking for all the world like some errant pre-schooler these older kids have been asked to look after.

Mandy uses her size well. Inside the school, she can knock me down with a well-placed hip-check as she walks by. Outside, she bulldozes right through me, turning and adding a kick or two for her audience's entertainment.

None of my friends understand it, but they, too, are cowed by her presence and too scared to intervene. She has turned on them as well, when they try to reason with her. The teachers, for some reason, turn a blind eye to the slowly escalating violence, which anyway mainly occurs when Mandy catches me at the far end of the playground alone, or in hallways filled with noisy kids running into their classrooms.

I come home with scraped knees and bruises, but when questioned at first, I am evasive, because my world has rules about tattle-tales. When I do finally break down and explain it, I find I have to account for the cause, but since I can't, my parents decide that this is one of those kid-things that I need to work out for myself. Am I sure that I didn't do something to offend her? Have I tried making friends with her?

When I come home with a black eye (after Mandy put an all-too-accurate elbow into my face as I passed by her out of the main doors) my father does phone the school to complain. Not surprisingly, he is met with the same answer he has given me: this is a kid-problem, let them sort it out for themselves. However, they do agree to 'talk to Mandy', which in turn simply makes my problem worse. Now, she has something on me and can claim a belated justification. More of her classmates join in.

****

One morning in November, I feel sick, but not in a way I can quite pin down. I just feel rotten, but my parents, believing I am trying to avoid school and the Mandy problem, have little sympathy, especially since I can't come up with even one identifiable symptom. Still, they let me stay home, although my mother warns me that she has a meeting plus a newsletter to put together, so I will have to amuse myself.

I spend the day curled up in bed. I don't eat. My mother does bring me some soup and toast at one point, but I am not hungry. I try to read, but the words squirm and blur on the page. I'm exhausted, I desperately want to sleep, but I don't seem to be able to manage more than fitful dozes, because I can't find a comfortable position to lie down in.

In the evening my father comes upstairs and says I need to get dressed. We have people coming for supper, and it would be rude, since I am obviously not truly ill, to avoid them. By this point, I feel so weak and disoriented that I don't even argue. I crawl out of bed, find some jeans and a tee shirt, and slowly go down to the dining room.

People around me are talking, but although I can hear them, I can't grasp any words. It all sounds both unnaturally loud and foggily muted at the same time, and suddenly, I can see the world contract into a narrow black tunnel where only the plate directly in front of me is still in focus.

I hear from a distance my own voice mumbling that I am sorry, I have to go back to bed, and then I am in the hallway at the foot of the stairs, and the black tunnel is suddenly narrower still, and I am reaching for the banister and watching it slowly, slowly, slowly fall away from me.

The next few hours are a kaleidoscope of odd, disjointed images. There is a circle of adult faces peering at me in consternation as I lie on the floor where I have fallen. There is my mother holding me close in the back seat of the car, and there is the vision of raindrops on the passenger side window, reflecting red traffic lights into tiny teardrop rubies. There is also the moment when I am in the X-ray room, and the technician is impatiently harassing me to stand up so she can take the shot. My mother tries to help me, but it's no use. My legs buckle and I'm on the floor in her arms, and she is giving the technician supreme shit in the vilest of gutter French.

I have pneumonia. I have apparently had it for at least three days, and it is the kind called 'walking' because the symptoms are subtler at this stage. I spend two nights in a bed in the children's ward, and there is, for the next few weeks, no desire I can voice that my parents do not move heaven and earth to fulfill.

****

After Christmas break, the weather is very cold and there's a ton of snow. Some days, even recess is held indoors, and when we do go out, we huddle in groups near the doors, unexposed and in clear view of the teachers. Indoors, I have become adept at avoiding being out in the open, hugging along the walls with a few other kids as protection. The Mandy problem fades into memory.

But in spring, it's as if the last months never were. In fact, months without a decent shot at me seem to have made her even more aggressive, and a new tactic emerges. Mandy and her friends link arms and cruise the playground chanting "We don't stop for nobody!" over and over, while running smaller kids like me down onto the ground. They aren't indiscriminate, and it is obvious to everyone I know that I am the ultimate target, every time. Safety lies in avoidance for all of us, but they enjoy this, too: knots of younger kids scattering in panic as they advance down, shouting their slogan.

I don't understand how the adults allow it. It's quite plainly mean, it's obvious we are getting hurt, but they just watch it without intervening.

Despite my best efforts to stay out of Mandy's way, there are occasional failures. I stopped to tie my shoelaces once, and got literally stomped over, winding up with a bloody nose[3]. And then, out playing a made-up game with a ball and some sketchy rules, I get caught alone by the marching phalanx of Mandy and Co., down near the baseball diamond.

It has been hot and dry, and I can feel the hard wire fencing of the backstop against my back, while the mocking chant gets louder and louder. Mandy is kicking at me, they're all kicking at me and raising up a cloud of dust, and all I can think is that this time, they aren't going to stop when I fall down, or cry, or bleed.

And I am close to tears, things are blurring, and then suddenly, very clearly, I look at the way their arms are hugging each other's shoulders and I feel my hands ball up into fists, and I am not scared – just incredibly, outrageously furious.

I hit Mandy squarely in the stomach, as hard as I possibly can.

She goes down with a weird huffing sound. She's crying. Her friends are shocked. I am still standing there, fists still out, looking at the rest of them, daring them to say or do anything, and they are staring back at me quite blankly, as if they aren't sure what they're doing there. One of them runs off to find the teacher who is supposed to be monitoring us at play.

And for reasons I will never understand, this time the

---

[3]To be completely fair to Mandy here: I got bloody noses at the drop of a hat in those days. Sometimes for no reason at all.

teacher gets involved.

****

I am suspended. I have to sit in the office until my mother comes. She has to go into the principal's office first and be talked to, and then she takes me home. She doesn't yell at me, or even question me about what I've done. Outside the school doors, she gives me a hug and says it will be okay, it's not the end of the world and that we don't have to talk about what I did right now, that it can wait.

At some point on the drive home, I manage to tell her my side of this, and she's good about it. My mom is a pacifist, but she says she understands how frustrated I got, and how angry, and while it wasn't right (or even a very good idea) she doesn't think the punishment fits the crime. She says that maybe this school, even though it is "open-plan" and stresses creativity, isn't as good for me as she thought it would be.

My father, when he gets home and she explains all this to him, is actually, I realize, a little amused and maybe even a little bit proud of me. He doesn't say so in words, but the corners of his mouth are tense in a funny kind of way and I know he is trying not to laugh.

After supper, when we are sitting around the living room with Ellis and his new girlfriend and a photographer friend who has just got back from Europe, my father gets a call from Mandy's father.

Mandy's father is very angry. I can hear the sound of his voice down the phone lines from right across the room, and it's a while before my dad can get in a word edgewise.

"Bill," says my dad, finally, "Have you seen my kid? She's only seven, and she weighs less than fifty pounds soaking wet."

My dad starts explaining about how long this has been going on, about the scrapes and the bruises, and the black eye, and says Bill can check because my dad called the school about that one.

And then I hear Mandy's dad so clearly that he could practically be in the room right there with us.

"Mandy! Get your sorry ass down here RIGHT NOW!"

****

The next day, the school phones. I technically am not suspended after all, although, because it is Wednesday by then, my mother lets me have an extra-long weekend and I don't go back to school till Monday.

Mandy gets the suspension instead, and her mother, very embarrassed, brings her to my house on Thursday afternoon and makes her apologize to me. It's not a very nice moment, because while Mandy did not like me before, I can see that she really, really hates me now.

The fallout from these events is bigger than that for me,

though. It's an instinctive thing – it's not as though I sit down and reason this out at all – it's just a sense of things. And that sense says that, love me as they do, my parents really have no idea how my life works and what challenges I face, and that I am, in some ways at least, on my own.

I am in tears and my parents are confused and not sure whether they should be angry or worried.

The French "fashion doll" Aunt Bessie sent me is broken. They know it is deliberate: her head has been cleanly removed and at the neck, her sawdust body has been meticulously, if inexpertly, re-sewn, and she was carefully replaced on her shelf, looking just fine until my mother swiped at her with a feather duster and the bisque head went flying.

They want to understand, but I can't seem to come up with the right words.

We played a lot of very complicated games, and this one was born out of some older kids studying "A Tale of Two Cities" in school and the chance airing of "The Scarlet Pimpernel" on TV one Saturday morning. Over three weeks, possibly more, we enacted various parts of our interpretation of the late seventeen hundreds.

It involved, among other things, building an all-too-efficient guillotine. We had just enough wit to grasp we could not actually cut Maddy Medvesky's head off (she insisted on being Marie Antoinette) so the doll had been drafted in as a replacement.

The discovery of the doll's sacrifice and the words "French

Revolution" are, to my child's mind, all the explanation that should be necessary.

My parents think that possibly I need professional help.

A Constant Sorrow

Life in my home operated on two basic principles: Benign Neglect and Books.

The first was the embodiment of the rule that unless something was obviously and immediately fatal or maiming, my parents' preference was to let me go ahead and do it, if I really felt I must. Not, of course, without discussion and warnings of the potential consequences. (That would have been irresponsible. Whatever other people viewing our lives from outside of the experience of living it may have thought, my parents took their role as parents quite seriously.) But they emphatically did not feel it was their job to wall me off from all experience or disappointment.

As a result, I learned early that failure hurts, but also that sometimes, things that people claimed were not possible turned out to be nothing of the kind. A thing might not be easy, and the results might not be what anyone could have reasonably expected, but that did not constitute 'impossible'.

Books were a different kind of rule. They were sacred. One never wrote in books, or let them be damaged willfully, although accidents from reading paperbacks in the bathtub were understood as inevitable occurrences.

Reading was one of the few activities that were not interruptible by less than earthshattering events. I could only defer chores around the house by claiming "Just till the end of the chapter, please, please, please?" – there wasn't anything else that was considered important enough that it could not be left till later.

The other point about Books was that my father firmly believed that there was almost no question I could pose that a book on the subject would not provide the answer for.

"If you want to learn to cook, get a cookbook."

When I came to questioning, in a general way, where babies came from, my parents ransacked the public library to find a book that could answer my need for knowledge in a way that did not confuse me or assign undue importance to the question. They found it in an easy-to-read volume that covered the entirety of how the human body's various parts were designed and how they functioned.

We read a chapter aloud each evening over a couple of weeks. Since the section on reproductive systems and pregnancy fell about midway through the book, it was presented to me not only as part of the natural and inherent function of all human beings, but also without the slightest bit of fanfare or moral opinions to confuse the issue.

Years later, my questions about money and economics resulted in a pile of heavy tomes by Friedman, Smith, Keynes and Galbraith.

But when I began to ask questions about The War, brought on by a discussion initiated at school by a teacher, who had then given us some hints of dire happenings but no details, my parents found themselves at a loss. Evasive explanations about why this particular conflict was elevated above the normal horrors of violent conflict and why, instead of the necessity of preventing war and advocating for peace, this war was unquestioned as to its utility and singular virtue, escaped my understanding.

In the early sixties, Anne Frank's diary notwithstanding, very little had been published on the subject that was suitable for a small child. My father tried to explain without terrifying me, but his guarded descriptions left me more mystified than ever, hampered as he was by parenthood and by his feeling that this was not really his story to tell. It was left to a friend of his to bridge the gap.

****

After World War Two ended, my father's natural aptitude for picking up languages[4] was drafted into service by an

---

[4] When my parents went to Japan, they spent fully two hours at Customs, because my father insisted on conducting the conversation in Japanese. The officials therefore kept asking him when he had *left* Japan, convinced no Caucasian could have learnt the language so thoroughly without having been raised there. My father kept reiterating that he had just arrived for his first visit, and tried to explain that he had gained most of his expertise through a book, a record and by taking classes in Kendo at the Japanese Cultural Centre in Toronto. Every Customs officer in the building came to have a look at the round-eye who could converse with such utter fluency in their language, and to examine his documents in hopes of finding some more palatable

organization one of his university professors was involved with, helping immigrants from Europe navigate the complexities of life in Canada. It was there that he met Nora Tomas, a young Hungarian Jew, and forged a friendship that lasted a lifetime.

Nora was an artist who lived in a studio in an ancient waterfront warehouse, supporting herself with sweetly sentimental paintings of native and Inuit children with fat rosy cheeks and stereotypical costumes. They were then turned into note-cards and small prints sold at all the major department stores, along with her tiny clay sculptures along the same lines. This stream of "artistic product" enabled her to work on enormous and challenging abstract canvases that were both inexplicable and awe-inspiring, to me at least, and were shown in economically unviable but politically orthodox galleries run by like-minded artists and patrons of all things iconoclastic and rebellious.

Every few months, Nora would come over and enjoy an alcohol-and-marijuana-charged evening of food and discussion, sleep in the guestroom and then collect me along with my PJs and toothbrush and we'd drive off to her place to spend the remainder of the weekend together. Nora let me mess about with real oil paints and with clay, agreed with me in preferring coffee and danish as a breakfast, and was, now that the time had come, willing to explain about The War.

---

explanation than "I taught myself". My mother was vastly amused.

It was shocking, all the more so because she rolled up her sleeve and showed me the tattooed numbers on her arm. She explained about the day the soldiers had come, the threats they'd issued to the villagers, and the way the villagers had turned on their friends and neighbours and told the soldiers which families were the Jewish ones.

She told me about the train journey, and her extended family, all of whom had perished, one way or another, mostly before the Liberation of the Camps. Her uncle had not survived the trip – he had already been ill with a fever when he was rounded up. She had not seen her mother, her grandparents or her two younger sisters since the day they had arrived and they had been led off to the euphemistic showers. Her brothers and her father did not make it through the first six months, and her aunt had died a few days after the Americans arrived, long enough to grasp that Hitler had lost, but too starved and brutalized to enjoy the news.

She described the conditions in the camps, and the terrible things she had seen, the things – such as sorting through the possessions of the dead after they'd been exterminated, and seeing what she was sure was her baby sister's embroidered blouse among the piles of clothing – that she had been forced to do. The things that she'd done to survive.

I don't know how she managed to explain all of this without scarring me beyond redemption[5]. I wept, to think of my beautiful Nora living through such agonies.

---

[5]Indeed, I am not sure she did manage this.

I wept for her family, and I was out of reason angry at the Christian villagers she had shared her life with, who had immediately given up the few Jewish families in their midst to the Nazis, apparently without a qualm.

Could they not have lied? Could they not have refused to tell? I demanded. Could they not have stood up to these monsters?

"No, no," Nora said. "They were terrified. They had their own families to think of. You can't blame people for being afraid."

Nora had wound up in a refugee camp after the Liberation, and it was there that another refugee woman who had a cousin in Toronto had decided to save Nora's life all over again. The people dealing with the refugees had decided, apparently, that without anyone in some other country to sponsor her, Nora might have to go back to Hungary. This was, in view of what she'd lost, a distinct non-starter for Nora. Not only was there nothing in Hungary for her to go back to, but the evil of the memories was still so fresh that it might have destroyed what little sanity she still possessed to do so.

But the woman she met in a line-up for getting some new clothes decided that since Nora's original, un-Anglicised last name was virtually identical to hers, they must be related – and therefore, her cousin was Nora's cousin.

Things were confused enough, Nora said, that the clerks accepted this relationship with little objection, and the

Toronto cousin did not seem averse to claiming Nora as a relative either. Nora arrived in Canada, spent one night with her non-related friends and then struck out to build her own new life.

She had, she said, been met with far more kindness, overall, than malice in her life. She did not blame ordinary people for behaving in ordinary ways. She was just grateful for those people who did more than the ordinary.

I was sceptical. My mother had taught me that evil was always to be confronted and resisted, and that civil disobedience was the greatest weapon one could wield against oppression.

But Nora pointed out that not everyone was suited to the crusader's life. It's up to you, she told me. It's you, who are brave, who can fight this fight, for everyone. It's you who will carry my memories forward and live the lessons we've learned. You're my hostage to the future.

I swore I would remember, always. I felt proud of her and of her trust in me. I don't know if she understood how, in that moment, I became as much her child as I was my parents'.

My mother likes a lot of music in her life, and so my father makes sure there is a way for us to listen to it everywhere. He buys a "hi-fi" for a room on the second floor that has nothing in it but walls of bookshelves crammed with encyclopedias, expensive art books and "the classics", a Persian carpet and a selection of enormous cushions my mother makes out of remnants of brightly coloured fabrics.

(And music, of course: towering stacks of LPs that grew to cover everything from the earliest folk music to the latest acid rock, with tangential forays into opera, classical music, jazz, and the blues.)

He also runs wires from the system to speakers in nearly every room, which necessitates drilling holes not only through the floorboards and wainscoting, but through the broadloom carpet in the hallway as well. When my grandmother hears about this, she is shocked and dismayed, but my father says only that it is his house and his carpet, and he guesses if he wants to drill holes in them, he can.

And when a good song comes on the radio, my mother grabs a broom and thumps the ceiling under my bedroom, so I can turn up my own tiny transistor radio and we can both sing along.

She Sells Seashells By the Seashore....

There is a terrible row going on at my house.

This fall, my father is 'on sabbatical' which means he is home a lot more, doing writing-and-research, and that Ellis, who moved to Canada to be my father's grad student but is done that and is a prof now, too, teaches his classes for him. It also means that some days, when I get home, there are pretty interesting things going on.

Today, my Oncle Jean, who is staying with us for a while, is with my dad out in the driveway, with tools spread out, working on Oncle Jean's car. I rush into the house, change into some jeans and go back out to help them.

Working on cars is terrific. I get to crawl underneath with them, and my dad has a flashlight to help see, and he and Oncle Jean explain about things. I get tools for them, and take care of the screws and gaskets and bolts, handing them back as needed. Grease drips on my face and clothes and I'm pretty happy.

What happens is that my grandparents come by, just as we are finishing up, and my grandmother starts yelling at my father about me being dirty and what am I doing learning about cars?

They go inside, and Oncle Jean and I are left to put away the tools. After that, we sit outside the garage for a while, awkwardly not talking about it, while he smokes a cigarette and I mope. After a bit, I say I am going in to change and he looks at me as if to say "Well, it's your funeral" but doesn't try to stop me.

The yelling is done: now my grandmother is speaking in a low, angry hiss about something called 'Services'. My grandfather kind of interrupts some, but she doesn't listen, she just goes right on hissing at my parents. My mother gives me a look and I slip away, upstairs to my room, shut the door tight and get out a book and try to ignore the fighting.

There's some door-slamming, and then a lot of grownup serious talking sounds. I can hear Oncle Jean in part of this, but I can't make out any words, mainly because I am trying not to.

Supper is tense. The Fields from next door have come over, and Molly and I talk to each other about cats and about Anne of Green Gables, which we both adore, while the grownups wait for us to be finished so we will go away and they can talk about whatever it is that they need to.

The talking goes on and on, long after I've gone to bed. There are phone calls, and low-voiced questioning sounds, and one time I hear my dad shout "Fuck it!" which is really bad. My father is not a shouter.

And then, when it is still dark out, my mother wakes me up. She still looks upset and worried, but she looks excited, too.

"Wake-up, Monkey-girl." That's one of my names. Officially it's 'The Rare and Elusive Monkey-girl' because we heard something like that on a nature program on TV, and my parents liked it. I have a lot of names, most of which do not appear on my birth certificate.

"Wake up! Time to pack!"

"Where are we going?"

"On an adventure," she says, laughing. We pack shorts and swimsuits, my favourite cotton play dresses, and tee shirts and pairs of jeans, and I later think that she must have had a plan for where we would end up because it all turns out to be the perfect things to bring.

In the driveway, Oncle Jean and Mr. Fields are there, helping my dad pack some camping things into the trunk. We have to shift the stuff they've already packed around a bit, because although the Buick is big, camping things take up a lot of space. There's not a lot of talking. Mr. Fields looks a bit grim, Oncle Jean looks amused, and my father looks like he would still like to hit someone.

The sun is still not properly up when we drive away. We don't stop, even after dawn, not even for breakfast. We don't go the way you go to drive to Algonquin Park, which is where we have always gone camping before. The signs say 'South', and that means we are going to Niagara Falls.

But we don't stop there, either. Instead we go past, to the signs for the Rainbow Bridge, which means we are going to The States.

I have been sort of lying down in the back, in a nest made up of pillows and sleeping bags, dozing a bit, but now I sit up. This is different. When we go to The States, my parents usually plan for it. It's got a Purpose: we go to Peace Fairs and to Civil Rights rallies. Important things. Work.

The border guard is friendly and disinterested. In thirty seconds we are past and whizzing down the highway, and suddenly everything is fine, my parents are laughing and making jokes, and we get to stop at a Howard Johnson's for breakfast.

We go first to Philadelphia, because my parents have friends there from Civil Rights. From there we go to another friend's, a family who are Quakers and live on a farm and who have daughters my age that I know from the Peace Fairs. We sell "Popcorn for Peace" for a nickel a bag, and we are good at it: we have learned how to look waifish and sweet so that ladies like us, and their boyfriends or husbands dig around in their pockets for nickels so as not to disappoint anyone.

Eventually, we end up at a house in South Carolina, outside a place called Myrtle Beach. The house is close to the shore, and it is owned by a woman named Martha. She inherited it from her grandfather. She says if her grandfather knew what kind of woman she would become, he would have left it to the cat foundation. This makes my parents laugh.

Getting anywhere on this trip had taken far longer than it should have, mainly owing to the family tradition of leaving no roadside attraction uninspected. We never fail to admire a scenic view or stop to be educated at a point of Historic Interest, and we wander off the main highways to follow signs to see toothpick houses, reptile zoos or the largest collection of garden gnomes in the world. We collect a souvenir from every place we can. The cheapest, tackiest and most garish is the goal, and we arrange the swaying hula-dancers, frog-shaped ashtrays, souvenir spoons and tiny, badly-painted plates proclaiming where we have been on the wide shelf behind the back seat. They fall down onto me whenever we have to brake suddenly, until my mother buys some Elmer's Glue and we set them permanently in place.

We also believe very firmly in eating at places where the restaurant is made to imitate something else, like a giant hot dog, or a fairy-tale mushroom, or a World War One airplane, and these are not always beside the highways. When you add to this the fact that my mother and I have never met a miniature golf course we did not instantly love, you can understand why it takes us over two weeks to get from a farm just south of Philadelphia down to Myrtle Beach[6].

Martha and her husband Rob live there with their son Emmet, and like our house, it is much bigger than they really need and so, like us, they are used to having people come and share it with them. The year before, when Dr. Ramirez from Madrid came to Toronto on an exchange,

---

[6]The distance, by the way, is exactly 599 miles.

his university did something wrong about his banking, and he arrived in Canada with nothing because Air Canada had lost his luggage. He and his wife and their baby were stranded and penniless. When they came to my father's office that first afternoon, Mrs. Ramirez said that Dr. Ramirez had not gotten a complete sentence out before my father said "Don't worry about a thing", cancelled a meeting with someone, and took them home to my mother. They stayed for six months, mainly because they were terrific fun, and my mother learned to make a lot of really interesting kinds of food.

So it's not at all strange to live with Martha and Rob and Emmet. Instead of school, my mother creates a project about the ocean for me to do, and I spend most of my days collecting information about the sea and the beach. I look up what kinds of sea-creatures live in the waters around Myrtle Beach and my mother loans me her camera so I can take careful pictures of seaweed and shells, to be identified from books later. I conduct experiments to test the reliability of the tide-charts and the changes in water temperature from day to day, and I read – and then write - stories and poems about the ocean.

When I'm not working on this, I help look after Emmet, who is only three. I teach him to tie his shoelaces, and to say the alphabet, and how to play tag and hopscotch. My mother makes Martha pleased by showing her how to make croissants and real French bread. Martha says my mother is "the shit" which my dad has to explain to me is a very big compliment.

After a few weeks, I have almost forgotten why we came here, when Cousin Leonard shows up.

I like Cousin Leonard a lot, although my mother says he is a lush, which means he drinks a lot, more than any other grownup I know. When he comes home to Toronto, he always stays for a couple of days at our house and organizes games of craps, which is gambling with dice, and tells me jokes I don't understand. Once, he got me to go around a room full of grownups asking if they wanted "Cigars? Cigarettes? Marijuana?" until my mother made me stop.

My parents weren't expecting him, and they are not very happy to see him this time. He talks in a very serious way to them and at one point, just after Martha calls through the screen door to the porch that she is starting dinner, Cousin Leonard looks at me and says,

"If nothing else, shouldn't she be in school?"

My mother pauses, hand on the handle of the door.

"Monkey-Girl, why don't you show Leonard what you've been doing?" And she goes inside.

I'm pretty happy to do this. I show him the photographs and the reading lists and my own poems I've written. There's quite a lot, arranged into separate exercise books for different parts of the project. When he leafs through the one that compares what the books say the temperature of the ocean here should be in October with my own temperature readings, he asks me why I did this. Why not just accept that the experts have already worked this out?

"It's the Scientific Method," I explain. My father says it is very important to understand the Scientific Method, and about Testing Your Theories. Without the Scientific Method, it is all just opinion and guesswork, and might not be The Truth.

When my mother comes back, Cousin Leonard smiles and says he gets her point.

My father brings beer from the grocery store. Cousin Leonard and he talk a lot, sitting on the porch and drinking the beer, until dinner is ready. My father says he understands that my grandmother is upset. He says that she is always upset, that she is a meddler, and also she is a word I'm not allowed to use, and Cousin Leonard agrees. But he points out that my grandfather would never let her do whatever it was that she had threatened to do. In fact, he tells my parents that my grandfather warned my grandmother that not only would he not pay for the lawyers she wanted, but "Would testify against her" and that they quarreled for days but my grandfather did not back down.

Cousin Leonard stays overnight, but after breakfast gets into his rent-a-car and goes back to Washington, where he works for the Canadian government, and a couple of weeks later, my parents agree that we could probably go home soon.

Things are never really the same between my father and

my grandmother. Before this, no matter how much my grandmother interfered and criticised and was rude, he was quiet about it and we arrived on most Sundays to join in the family Sunday dinners. After Myrtle Beach, we went much less often, sometimes going as long as two or three months without any contact at all. When we did go, he was less tactful, and did not miss a chance to say sarcastic things to her.

****

I'm not sure exactly when I realized that the dynamic in my father's family was not normal. One becomes accustomed to what *is*, as a child, and you just accept it.

My grandmother was a twin[7]. Her sister was as much a fixture in my life as my grandmother was – I saw her in all of the same places, which consisted of church and those inevitable Sunday dinners.

When my great-grandfather died, it was discovered that he had split his daughters' inheritance in two. There was the business, which went to Aunt Ann, and the properties, which went to my grandmother. They were only twenty when he died, and instantly, each assumed that the other had gotten the better deal. They'd quarreled bitterly, even before the funeral.

My great-aunt Ann and her husband came every Sunday for the dinners, but she and my grandmother did not

---

[7] Annabelle and Arabelle. Annabelle was just 'Ann' but inexplicably, my grandmother was called 'Birdie'.

speak to each other; they had not exchanged a single word directly to each other since the day of their father's funeral in 1921. They communicated through their husbands or anyone else who was there ("Harry. Tell Her to pass the salt."), and left alone together, I imagined that they sat in angry silence, mouths firmly shut and both constitutionally unable to retrieve any object situated too close to the other twin.

Despite this, they were united in their righteous condemnation of their younger sister, my Aunt Bessie. They came as close as they ever would to a conversation when one of Bessie's letters arrived and was read out by some neutral third party.

About a year before my great-grandfathers' death, sixteen-year-old Bessie had done the unthinkable and run off with a much older, married man.

Forty years on, both of her sisters still talked in hushed, shocked tones about 'that hussy'. It must have been like a bomb going off in an upper-class and rigidly rules-bound Toronto household in the 1920s. Bessie received what was, in my grandmother's and my great-aunt's considered opinion, the only fitting treatment of instant disinheritance, utter abandonment and the pronouncement from her father To Never Speak Her Name Again. His death mitigated this only a little, in that her older sisters could now gossip freely on the supposed fate in store for little sister Bessie.

This eagerly awaited forecast of the natural punishment, that Bessie would end up penniless, alone and dying of some dreadful disease in a gutter, did not materialize. Perhaps out of pure mischief, Bessie began a primarily one-sided correspondence with her family, so that they were aware of every important stage of her life thereafter. Her lover eventually obtained a divorce, married Bessie, moved with her to England and in due course, when he died, left her a tidy little fortune that against many odds had been preserved through the Crash of '29, a sequence of events that utterly infuriated her two older sisters.

A couple of years later, Bessie married again, to a much richer, even older man, who did not survive the London Blitz, thus enlarging Bessie's wealth once more. This further enraged her sisters, who openly questioned the wisdom of their Creator. During the war, Bessie joined the war effort to become a driver, navigating the darkened streets of London and beyond, ferrying generals and colonels and occasionally, a politician or two, and, to hear her tell it, she enjoyed herself hugely.

In the postwar era, she found herself still in possession of a considerable fortune, and embarked on the exciting career of being a wealthy widow who could please herself. Periodically, she would descend upon the Toronto enclave, wearing beautifully made, extremely fashionable clothes, where her dyed, platinum blonde hair, expert make-up and her lifted, toned and rigorously-schooled body caused indignant eye-rolls from every woman over twenty-five, and private anguish in her sisters' more matronly bosoms.

For my own part, Bessie was the only one of the three

of them that I cared for in any deep way. She was outrageous and funny with her stories of war-time hijinks that even my male relatives who had served could not seem to match for daring and humour. Moreover, she smoked Russian cigarettes in an elegant ebony and silver cigarette-holder, spoke in French to my mother as a gesture of solidarity against "The Family", and periodically sent me wildly inappropriate and extravagant gifts: the antique French 'fashion doll', a faux-zebra-skin catsuit, the first Beatles LP, a box of Mary Quant eye paints.

It was assumed by her sisters that Bessie continued in her wicked ways ("Affairs", my grandmother said darkly once, after a particularly double-entendre laden missive had arrived from London) so it was a bit of a surprise when she announced she had remarried once more, this time to a much younger, utterly penniless man she had met at a ski-resort in Switzerland.

His name was Bob. He was English, fair, very good-looking, and loathe as I was to agree with my grandmother on anything, more than ordinarily dim. My grandmother referred to him as B'B – claiming he wasn't bright enough to merit an entire syllable - but as always, the fascination with Bessie's wicked life precluded any suggestion that she would not be welcomed home, after a fashion.

The family opinion was that B'B was a gigolo, that he knew what side of his bread was buttered, that he had only married Bessie for money, and that she would Rue The Day.

But Bob adored Bessie. When they came through on their way to skiing in Banff, or to visit acquaintances in Vancouver, every plan he made revolved around her likes and dislikes, with her comfort as his only aim. He went out early each morning to bakeries that sold the kinds of pastries she liked for breakfast. He remembered the scarves and sweaters in case she got chilly, even on warm days. He made sure, before he ever went off to watch wrestling matches or baseball games (Bob was adamant that televised sports was utterly inferior to "the real thing"), that every need and desire of Bessie's was considered and attended to.

Her death left him inconsolable and heartbroken, and the enormous amount of money she had left him turned out to mean nothing. He bought a tiny seaside cottage in Cornwall, spent nearly nothing at all, and died himself, two years later, leaving everything to a charity for Wayward Girls.

My family is not very good about time. We are frequently late, and occasionally miss trains, even airline flights, and this time, we nearly miss my uncle's wedding.

We just make it, though, sprinting past the bride as she's stepping out of her father's car, and scrambling into the first seats we can find, gasping and out of breath.

At some point, the priest who has agreed to solemnize this union decides to give a little dissertation on marriage, speaking sonorously of the give and take, the ebb and flow of life together.

"Eb and Flo?" my father says to us. "Isn't that a vaudeville act in the Catskills?"

"The famous tap dance twins," my mother agrees.

We are not the only ones now doubled up trying to stifle hysterical giggles, though.

Sins of the Fathers

Part of every summer was spent at the family cottage in Muskoka country. At least some of it was timed to give us a few happy, unencumbered days where it was only we three, or, at most, my grandparents as well, who uncharacteristically tried to leave us alone, perhaps because socially, my parents were a bit of an embarrassment for them. There was swimming and diving off the dock, learning to row boats and paddle canoes, and fishing, and going into the tiny town nearby for ice-cream cones, and I mostly remember those days with pleasure.

My grandfather always took umbrage with the entire concept of inheritance taxes, and wound up finally subdividing the enormous lakefront acreage into smaller blocks, one for each set of us. Somehow, through some complicated process of deeds and titles, they were successfully transferred while remaining "in the family", a kind of co-op deal or the creation of some kind of property trust. My parents immediately chose the lot furthest and most inconveniently situated in relation to the original house and built an A-frame chalet, a small boathouse and a really good dock with lots of space to hang out at.

I don't like my cousins much. I am too small and too young and too much unlike them to defend myself from their ideas of "fun", but since it has always been this way, I don't completely recognize that they aren't really very nice or very happy children. I just think of the few days where our presence at the cottage overlaps as one more inexplicable thing I need to put up with, till one set of us goes home.

The A-frame took two years to finish, but by the second summer, it is tantalizingly close: the windows and doors are in, and most of the flooring, and you can see where the kitchen and bathroom will be, once the water and sewage systems get done.

Today is very hot and it seems it has sapped the aggression from my cousins. We roam the property in something approaching accord, searching for cool shady places, because even swimming is exposing us to the hot, hot sun and we just can't find a happy medium there. Eventually, we end up at the far end, where the dirt road runs out and we can see the A-frame through the trees.

There isn't really a decision, we just wander towards it. Jenny, who is the eldest, she wants to see it, I guess, and we troop in. Becky, who is youngest and likes to play house a lot, wants to know where the bedrooms will be, and where we will put our dishes. I can hear a lot of giggling and thumping footsteps as Christopher and Jenny run up and down the newly installed stairs of the front deck, where my mother says we will have barbecues. Then Becky wanders off and I look around to make sure everything's the same as when we came, because my dad gets upset if tools or two-by-fours go missing.

Just as I reach the door, it slams shut, and there is Christopher, grinning like a maniac, waving the door-key and laughing. They are all laughing, and then, just as suddenly, they are gone.

I know, though, they haven't gone far. The point of this is to make me angry, to make me yell, to make me plead to be let out. I am just well enough acquainted with the general tone of their amusements to decide that it will be over sooner if I refuse to do that, so that they will get bored with this game.

Only, no one comes back.

I find an old newspaper and force myself to sit quietly and read everything in it, including some very dull things about baseball teams. I close my eyes and count extremely slowly to one hundred, once in English and once in French. I climb up the temporary ladder to the loft part, where my parents will have their room, and try to see through the trees out the back window, where I am sure my cousins are hiding. There is no sign of anyone. I curl up in a pool of sunlight, feeling awkwardly strange and unhappy, and I must have dozed, because after a bit, the sunlight has moved a long way away from where I am.

And now it occurs to me that they have no intention of coming back at all. There is a queasy feeling inside me and I want to cry, but I don't because that's a baby thing, and I am emphatically not a baby anymore.

I climb back down to the main room and check the door: it is still locked. I peer out into the fading afternoon, trying to listen harder, see farther, but there is nothing there but a mild breeze and the soft sound of little wavelets on the lake.

I am suddenly frightened. No grownups know where I am, and I realize that my cousins won't dare tell. It could, I think, be days before anyone thinks to look here. I am already hungry – I think I could starve to death here and suddenly I am crying, screaming, begging, rattling at the locked front door in pure panic.

It is nearly dark when I have exhausted myself, and am sitting in a huddle on the floor, looking up at the door and wishing for some magical moment when Chris will reappear and let me out, or envisioning trying the door for the hundredth time and discovering it was only stuck, not locked. But I realize this won't happen. I am through the panic and into a cold, hard, angry place, and that makes me consider a plan I would not have, even an hour ago, ever dreamed of.

In the back is the stack of tools, and I find the biggest hammer there. I walk back to the front room of the A-Frame, which is all big glass windows so we will have hours of morning sunlight every day, and I quite deliberately smash in the window closest to me.

It takes three good blows to make a real hole worth speaking of, but on that third try, the glass suddenly explodes into a spiderweb of breakage with a fist-sized hole at the centre. And although I try to be careful, I cut my hands and my arms in a few places, pulling out enough of the glass to squeeze through. None of the cuts are very bad, but there is some blood. I am oblivious – I am feeling quite triumphant, and nothing about this bothers me until I reach the big house, out of breath from running the whole way.

All the grownups are very, very angry. I have missed supper, and made them worried. And when I stammer out a vague explanation of being locked in the A-frame and having to break the window, my father absolutely loses it and shouts at me, which is almost a first in my memory. He doesn't understand how I could have been locked in and I can't tell him, not least because now I am scared and near tears, and my mother is not helping because she is upset at seeing the blood dripping from my arm, and my uncle is being nasty about Discipline and Manners and The Way I Am Being Raised.

"Jenny made Chris throw away the key."

Becky is too young to know about the laws of the playground, and she has a nasty streak anyway, you can tell she is enjoying the reaction she gets here. And Jenny and Chris have gone from secret smirking to open-mouthed shock, and everyone except my mom is suddenly very quiet.

I wind up in my parents' room, where my mother cleans up my cuts. My dad brings me a sandwich and a big mug of hot chocolate, and when my mother has gone to find my PJs and toothbrush, he gives me a very big hug and apologizes.

"I should have known you wouldn't do this on purpose, kidlet. I should have tried listening instead of yelling, and I'm sorry."

When I get up the next day, everyone is very nice to me, even my grandmother, who is usually one long complaint about my hair, my clothes and my table manners. I get to take the rowboat out by myself, all the way to the sandbar and back, and no one tells me I am rowing wrong, even when I scrape the paint off tying it up at the dock.

****

Fast forward a few years.

One hot July night my parents go off to dinner and some dancing with friends[8], and I am curled up with a book in the main room of the A-frame, with the transistor radio picking up a local rock station playing the same six songs in succession, when there's banging at the door.

I am surprised to see Jenny and Chris. Since the summer of the broken window, Jenny and I have been distant and scrupulously polite, while avoiding each other as much as possible, although Chris occasionally comes around to our dock and is 'acquaintance-friendly' for brief periods before going back to my uncle's place.

Jenny smiles through the screen door and waves an unlit joint at me, so I let them in.

---

[8]In addition to city socializing and attending the same schools, almost everyone I knew had cottages in the same general area, and summers were just endless weekends with better weather than at home.

"It's murder up at our place," Jenny says. "Sandy is weeping non-stop, the baby never stops screaming and Dad's gone off the deep end about Becky's marks at school. World War Three. Had to get out, you know? And Chris said, well, he said..."

"I said if she brought a peace offering and promised not to be a bitch, you might be willing to let us hang around for a while."

"What's Sandy crying about?" I ask, because I really don't have a response for this piece of fraternal honesty.

Sandy is the new aunt. My uncle has had four wives now, and a child from each. Sandy was very smiley and chatty and young and pretty at the wedding, but she looked years older, very tired and much grimmer at the last Sunday family supper I was at, just after the baby was born.

"God, being married to him is enough to cry about, isn't it?" says Jenny, and I grasp that she's right, although I'm not sure why.

We smoke the joint. Jenny is holding forth on life and high school, as if this was an experience peculiar and unique to her. Chris seems to have passed out on the floor.

When she runs out of words to describe her teachers (all male, all either sexy beyond belief or senile washouts, "It's unbelievable any of them ever found the frumps they married" and none of them know anything about anything) and has delivered a polemic on the uselessness of university since my uncle won't let her go anywhere but University of Toronto, and all she wants is to get the hell away, she looks at Chris, sleeping peacefully with his head on a cushion and remarks that she isn't interested in dragging him back up the road.

"He was blind drunk by suppertime," she says, and I foolishly ask why.

"Dad beats the crap out of him," she says, as if this is a perfectly ordinary thing that I should have known about.

At the door, Jenny stops and turns, and looks searchingly at me and says, awkwardly,

"I'm sorry about your mom being sick. She's okay, your mom."

I shut the door behind her, without a word.

"Jesus Fuck, I thought she'd never leave," says Chris, now sitting up and looking remarkable sober.

Our eyes lock.

"He hits her too," he says, offhandedly. "And worse. But not so much anymore. He's got Sandy, now. And Becky, too, pretty much, I guess."

Although Jenny behaves as if the evening never occurred, Chris and I become friendlier. Back in the city, he will unexpectedly show up at my place with bottles of whiskey or hash oil doobies, and behaves the way I think a baby brother might have done.

Queen's Park is where we are in sunshine, wreathed in incense, enveloped by sudden music, among friends we do not know. There is dancing and there are flowers, and because even the cops are kind of naive and inexperienced, the aroma of marijuana seems to drift unnoticed amid the trees.

My father's hair is longer now, and my mother has her hair caught back by a braided rainbow of ribbons like a birthday gift, and on my cheeks, Nora renders paisley curls of colour on my face, and I listen to the wind and the faint echoes of laughter.

In the evening, or some other evening like it, there are people in our living room, somnolent and reeking of patchouli or vibrantly awake and discursive, exploring everything from the nature of mortality to the colour of the curtains. One friend, a writer and historian, declares — in connection with what, I do not know — that "Proust was a colossal bore".

My mother immediately christens him "Marcel" and this is so indelibly inked into my child's mind that four decades later, watching him being interviewed on TV, I am momentarily confused by his actual name scrolling along the bottom of the screen.

Better Living Through Chemicals

My theme song for the whole of 1968 is "Suite Judy Blue Eyes". It runs through my life like an audio river, encapsulating everything I love about my life. It is colour and pattern, it is dance, it is endless summer sunlight and velvet night, it is the magic of being able to recognize your allies by the length of their hair and the beads around their necks. It is the mystery of boys and the nascent solidarity of "women's lib", it is the sense that the world can change if we want it to. It is late night serious discussion, it is acid trips and temple bells, it is like wine for the soul.

The change in our lives was gradual at first: it came on the heels of new folk songs and a rocking, raucous British invasion, both speaking directly to *now*, instead of harking to a simpler past. Instead of black skirts and berets, my mother slowly introduced us to a rainbow that became a crazy patchwork swirl of printed muslin from India paired with peasant blouses stiff with embroidered designs. My father exchanged his grey flannel trousers and corduroy jacket for jeans and a t-shirt with Che Guevara's portrait silkscreened in red. Peace Fairs became Be-Ins, dancing became as natural as breathing, and paisley became my doodle of choice, in every margin of every piece of paper I came into contact with.

It was a nearly seamless transition – we left nothing crucial behind. Politics still mattered. Standing up and being counted at demonstrations, working, writing, speaking for peace and liberation, that all was still there. It just came now with a sense that we were not alone, that these values were shared with a wider world, that we could achieve what had only a few short years before seemed like impossible dreams.

It got married to *joy*. Suddenly, demonstrations and rallies were less "work" and more like parties. You went almost as much to be with your friends as to express your politics – this only seemed frivolous or evanescent to people outside this sudden revolution of style wedded to purpose because they had not experienced the desolate aloneness of political activism before the transfusion of hippiedom. The crowds swelled, and the music, the dancing, the colours all reinforced the belief that this time, the world could change.

There were bumps.

My father is reprimanded for quietly but determinedly advising, aiding and abetting students to create protests against the magnificently cavalier attitude that the university has about furnishing a relevant education to its students. Specifically, he told them how to circumvent the minimal security in order to stage a sit-in protest, and as a result, there is a sort of hearing, a patronizing "talk" and veiled threats, although a friend in the biology faculty points out that this is all pretty meaningless, because my dad has tenure. Getting rid of him would be amazingly complicated.

As a response, he grows his hair longer, wears ever more colourful outfits, and wangles a seat on a committee trying to negotiate a better set of curricula guidelines that accept the idea that maybe just delivering sets of orthodox opinions set out as "fact" is not the only or best way to educate anyone.

There were the long stints of hospitalization for my mother as doctors tried to find chemical and surgical solutions to the time-bomb ticking inside her. But there were also the months of remission when new clothes got created, when we got to concerts as an intact family, when we marched and rallied together for peace.

My parents, working against the current of popular beliefs as always, opted for truth where my mother's condition was concerned. My mother felt that not telling me would be tantamount to a betrayal: two days after the "second opinion" diagnosis confirmed her death sentence, they sat me down to explain the realities. The doctors, always overcautious, had murmured and jargonized and settled on three months, maybe six, even a year if the drugs did what they should.

My parents stressed that this was all conjecture, really. It was possible that it could be longer – my mother particularly felt more confidence in her survival at that point, and in this she was quite correct. From diagnosis to deathbed turned out to be three years.

Meanwhile, changes had to be made.

The one that concerned me came around six months along, when the true nature of the cycle of remission and hospitalization revealed itself. The end of remission could be brutal and sudden and it disrupted everything. My parents found that the effect this had on me was not good, and they decided, regretfully, to send me away to a boarding school. I argued, I wept, I attempted emotional blackmail. They weren't unmoved, but they were quite firm.

Being eleven, I missed a salient point, missed it so completely that I was nearly thirty years old before I recognized it.

They had expected decades together, my mom and dad. They had expected time enough for all the experiences they wanted to share, and this was being torn away from them without the slightest chance of reprieve. Much as they loved me, they needed to cram an entire marriage into the months they had left, and this must have seemed like the best way to do it without shortchanging me completely.

Not surprisingly, the "school" they chose was exactly the opposite of what anyone else's definition of boarding school would have been.

Willowrun offered itself as a farm environment educational "experience", with teachers operating as "facilitators" and children being encouraged to be full participants in every aspect of how things were run[9]. It

---

[9]This wasn't my first foray into being dragooned into having curriculum or organizational "input". These occasions took the form of seminar-style meetings, where adults asked what we thought was missing from our school experience. Since our answers, when pushed, tended to be "More art" or "More

had the additional incentive of being less than a two-hour bus ride from downtown Toronto, and it was agreed that since my circumstances were slightly different than most other students', I would go home on most weekends so that even if my mother was in hospital, we would have some reasonable amount of time together.

****

In the end, I wound up loving Willowrun. Everyone was aware of what was going on in my life, and while I never felt pushed into discussion, I did feel free to occasionally unload my fears and sorrows onto adult people, when it all got to be too much to hold inside.

I was also introduced to farm chores, and inoculated forever against romanticizing rural life. One got assigned tasks that simply had to be done. Feeding chickens was the first one I got, paired up with Jessie who with her brother had been at the school from its inception. I learned a number of ugly truths about chickens (ie: they could be hypnotized by drawing a line in the dirt and pushing their heads down to it, where they became cross-eyed and mesmerized until we had cast out all the feed and – little savages that we were – we then kicked them ungently off the lines). I learned to milk cows, and also how to wake up at the crack of dawn to do it. I discovered that weeding was not something I would ever be good at: my ability to distinguish one kind of green

---

recess", followed by "More sports", the meetings were generally not successful, and in the end, the adults did whatever they had wanted to do to begin with.

shoot from any other is minimal, even today.

Yes, it was exactly what you are thinking: a hippie commune masquerading as a vaguely school-like entity. Jessie and Josh were there while their parents wandered the globe in search of enlightenment. One of the adults was there because he had been abandoned by his wife for an entire rock band, and spent a lot of time alone, building over-engineered and utterly indestructible wooden fences along the property lines of the farm. There was a couple from New Zealand, both licensed to teach[10], who came without warning one day, along with two children under school age, and seemingly without discussion were absorbed into the mix. There was Alison, who was fourteen and whose parents had dumped her there one weekend the year before during some kind of "family emergency", to be picked up on the Monday. They were never heard from again.

And then there were a dozen or so kids like me, whose parents were looking for a school that would not crush their children into dust, who perhaps had hopes that skills in agriculture and living with others would equip their children better than memorizing multiplication tables, or who just disbelieved in the need for formal education of any kind. My parents had always vigorously augmented my school life with books, discussion, more books and a wide variety of first-hand experiences. This was on the assumption that school was bound to be

---

[10]There were real teachers, accredited insofar as the requirements in Ontario were at the time. They had a very hands-off approach, but if you did show signs of wishing to learn something, they proved extraordinarily good at teaching it.

inadequate by definition, since neither of them had fond memories of their own school days. From that standpoint, Willowrun was an inevitable choice.

Maggie and her husband Bill, who had inherited the land and decided to start the school, were also teachers, which was why Willowrun existed as a "school". They had pretty high ideals and lofty goals and so on, but neither of them had grown up in the country. The first year, I gathered from bits of reminiscence, had been very difficult.

By the time I arrived, they had gotten a fair hold on the mechanics of daily country life, and had even gotten to the point where they could sell some of our produce to the burgeoning health food restaurant business, mostly centred in Toronto.

A massive donation of books from a nearby estate being liquidated arrived around the same time as I did, and Jessie and I volunteered to help go through them and sort out and shelve them in the shed that had been built as a "library". Ryan, the male half of the New Zealand couple, was nominally in charge of this but lost interest within a week, distracted by one of the boys discovering a passion for botany.

Jessie and I, having become addicted to the serendipitous nature of the task, soldiered on. We were rewarded by finding a huge collection of science fiction paperbacks – everything from Asimov to Zelazny – and since no one was really paying attention to what we were or were not accomplishing, we stopped for several weeks to read them all.

After that, we found a respectably broad and not completely unscholarly selection of history books, and worked our way through the parts of past world events that we liked best. Slightly risqué books about various English queens and overly-general treatments of escapades like Schliemann's search for Troy seemed to predominate, and only one book out of several boxes' worth even mentioned the Americas.

By the time we'd exhausted the donation's reading potential and organized the books into neatly shelved and labeled categories according to our eleven-year-old tastes and whims, it was springtime, and my mother still lived.

One of the more sacred principles at Willowrun was the idea that the traditional dividing line between teachers and students was an arbitrary concept, that we all "taught each other". When Alison discovered that I spoke French, she decided that I should teach her to speak it as well. Once she got a reasonable vocabulary going, it was a bit like a secret code, and it created a strange bond between us: not exactly friendship, but a sort of alliance against an inexplicable world we neither of us understood properly. And so, as a kind of payment for services rendered, Alison gave me a hit of LSD for my twelfth birthday[11], with the advice that I only take half, being new to this. I split the hit, therefore, with

---

[11]Yes, shocked gasps all around. Look, I don't recommend this as a normal practice. But it wasn't really that uncommon an occurrence at the time.

Jessie.

We took it around 7 o'clock or so, just after the big communal supper in the main house. I was unconcerned. Lots of people I knew had done acid, and talked about it. I had some hazy ideas of what was probably going to happen, and I felt only mild, pleasant anticipation.

There is no describing something like this. The start was weird-feeling, but not upsetting – just a kind of swooshing up into a state of imbalance.

At some point, Danny came into the front yard where we were clinging to the fence-posts. We had been tripping out on the sound of our own names, hooting them out into the darkness, and were now giggling at nothing. I don't know if Alison had told him what was happening or if he just knew instinctively, but he decided to take charge of us.

Danny wasn't a student, exactly, and he wasn't, technically, a teacher. He was a local boy who had heard about the crazy hippies trying to do some kind of commie "back to the land" thing up the road from his parents' place, and wandered by to check it out one day. Appalled by the total lack of knowledge exhibited by the half-dozen original participants, he'd offered some suggestions, shown them a few tricks, and come back a few days later to see how things were going. He kept turning up, sometimes with cast-off tools lifted out of some friend or relation's back shed, and always with solutions to problems no one at Willowrun had ever imagined existed.

He'd listened, too, and asked questions, on subjects that weren't covered by the local high school he attended. He borrowed some books, stuck around for some meals, shared a few joints. And one day, he just stayed on, appropriating a small cabin on the other side of the main yard, and acting as a kind of live-in agriculture expert as well as an informal liaison between Willowrun and the surrounding local farm families.

We adored him, as only pre-adolescent girls can, but then, everyone liked Danny. He was strong, monosyllabic, musically talented and utterly dependable.

There was a small hitch along the way across the yard when, having suddenly marveled at the way walking was accomplished, Jessie forgot how to do it, and had to be half-cajoled and half-carried, hilariously, the rest of the distance.

Now ensconced in Danny's cabin, we explored the new world.

It was glorious fun.

It was all colours and patterns and even the tiniest, most mundane things became utterly engrossing. I was particularly entranced by the design on the window curtain, a scrap of red-on-red brocade fabric usually seen on someone's granny's sofa cushions, which now moved in endless curls and twists, a slow-motion whirlpool that never quite found its centre point.

Suddenly, everything in the world seemed clearer, more real and completely logical on some level I had never grasped before. When I closed my eyes, the same curtain patterns morphed and collided into explosions of new colours and shapes, pulsing to the music that Danny was picking out on his guitar. Periodically, he made tea, and read us poetry, until we noticed the lightening sky, and went out to watch the sun rise over the sheep pens.

Having sent us off to our own beds, it must have been noticed that Danny was the one who milked the cows that morning. Alison grinned conspiratorially at us over the supper-table that evening, and Maggie looked slightly worried, but no one ever discussed it with us.

I had turned on and tuned in. There was, obviously, nothing for me to drop out of, though.

My father is standing in the hall and laughing so hard he drops the telephone receiver.

In Washington, at a huge protest rally, my mother has been arrested.

For hitting a cop with her sign.

She is out of jail when she phones, and at the airport on her way home. She called Cousin Leonard, of course, when the police let her have "her phone call", and because he has always kept his mouth firmly shut about the people he plays poker and drinks with, he has favours he can cash in. The paperwork about her arrest disappears on condition that she just go quietly back to

Canada and try not to hit any more cops.

My mother is a pacifist. She maintains, always, that she had no intention of hitting anyone, that she was merely maneuvering her sign, trying to tuck it under her arm, to help another person who had tripped and fallen, and that the end of the sign just happened to graze the cop standing over someone he was beating with a night stick. An accident.

Other witnesses differ. She belted a cop, hard, with a protest sign.

For peace.

Funeral Games

The day of my mother's memorial service is typically November in Toronto; it is cold, grey and damp, although it does not actually rain until the next morning. Despite the shared purpose, we devolve into knots of people defined by our relationships or lack thereof.

My father's family arrives impeccably dressed in sober greys and blacks and they hug themselves to themselves. My mother's family is hovering by the entrance-way, supported by their own numbers and by longtime close friends.

There is a huge crowd of people from the various political groups, much less formally attired, who merge and reassemble among themselves. There are three nuns and a soon-to-be-defrocked priest who became family friends after taking a class from my father. All four had then been recruited into the antiwar movement out of sheer admiration for my mother's passion and commitment, and gone on to become well-known organizers with impressive arrest records.

There is a surprisingly large group of nurses and doctors who only came to know her these last three years, but have taken time off work to say goodbye, even so.

Look: no amount of time eases this. My mother died before I could know her as one woman to another, and that is a pain that can't be measured.

Still, she filled me, especially in those final months, with all the wisdom and advice she could. She must have known I understood very little of what she said to me, but she knew too, somehow, that it would reach me eventually, when I needed it.

There were moments on that day that are worth remembering, no matter how painful. My father had asked me to read Matthew Arnold's "Dover Beach", and I manage not to cry by imagining that I am perched beside her on a rock near the sea at Myrtle Beach, listening as she recites it to me for the first time.

He chose Elizabeth Barrett Browning's classic. There probably wasn't anything he could have chosen that would have been easier, but still, he didn't make it completely through. My grandpére stood up and in a strong, heavily accented voice finished it with him. And still, I did not weep.

At home, the place is crammed with people. My grandmére has gone to bed, armoured with Vallium and guarded by my Tante Céline. The women on my father's side of the family attempt to make a case for going through my mother's things – right then and there, apparently – and this causes a pretty acrimonious exchange with my grandpére, who has the advantage of being able to swear in two languages. I manage, barely, not to laugh.

There are relatives who hardly know me and who certainly knew my mother less, who somehow manage to combine disapproval and irrelevant advice with attempts at condolence. Some of them, for unfathomable reasons, give me money, as well. I manage not to openly rage.

There are people I've known all my life who are trying to let me know they are there, that they want to help. There is nothing in this world approximating help for this, I think. But I don't weep for them, either.

There is my father. It is beyond tears.

I am saved, literally and figuratively, though, by the small army of my friends that develops within minutes of the news getting around. They stay with me for days, a little band of emotional troopers ready to face down the world for me. They begin to vet everyone who telephones or comes to talk to me, sizing up how much damage the mourner might do, and how much of that damage I can take without breaking right then and there. And for weeks afterwards, they make sure of me, till they are convinced that some kind of healing has begun, that it has taken hold, that I will make it through. They shoulder the task of outward mourning, they cushion me from memories by making new ones, they build a safe place for me to escape the sadness and they wait it all out patiently, till I learn how to at least fake some happiness for them and set us all free.

****

Christmas was always a big deal for my family. My mother might not have believed in the God of the Catholic Church (or any other conventional definition of "god", for that matter), but she knew what joy was and how to expand it, how to transmute it into a living thing. Any occasion would do, but Christmas made it easy.

Preparations began after Halloween (another favourite holiday) and inched its way through carefully orchestrated stages to a crescendo of barely-contained excitement and anticipation; a stringing together of traditional customs and zany, goofy rituals she created, into a seamless fabric of happiness.

There were coloured-paper and threaded popcorn-and-cranberry chains and handmade wooly socks in red and green that joined with Santa Claus traps [12], rewritten Christmas carols, and stories featuring our own imagined characters, "The Christmas Piglets" [13].

There was the annual and always theatrically overdone production of whatever Shakespeare play, ancient fairy tale or historical event my mother felt inclined to that year, invitations to which evenings were much sought after by friends, and then it was strangely echoed by attending Midnight Mass on Christmas Eve.

---

[12] These were mousetraps, carefully decorated with glitter and ribbon, and baited with bits of candy cane. When I was very small, my mother would spring the traps after I was in bed, and use my father's galoshes to make ashy footprints leading from the fireplace to the tree and back again. Apparently, I went utterly insane with joy at the sight of this on Christmas morning.

[13] I can't describe this. Trust me: they were loud, vulgar, lovable and occasionally sort of gross.

There was the deliciousness of tortierre, sweet potato pudding and turkey with sage stuffing, the magic of Japanese oranges, the heady sweetness of chocolate Santas, the buzz of Secret Projects and the sudden arrivals of long-lost friends from parts unknown.

And then, there was The Day itself which never disappointed, and there were all the days leading up to it that created a sense of both chaos and order, equally amazing in their turn. It was, in short, the best time of the year because she made it so.

****

Less than two weeks after the disaster-day of the memorial service, my father came upstairs where I was listlessly trying to understand why the comedian on Ed Sullivan wasn't funny, and announced that we'd be spending Christmas in the Bahamas.

We left a full ten days before Christmas, having only barely coped with the seasonal mood around us, flying out of a chilly Toronto first to Miami, where we spent four hours smoking cigarettes and perusing magazines, and then to Nassau, collapsing in a nondescript hotel for one night before getting onto a rather ramshackle boat that deposited us on an island called Eleuthera.

I don't know why or how my father picked it. I don't know what he told the staff at the hotel. I know that we had a lovely pair of rooms, that everything was hot and brilliantly coloured, and that despite the fact that I was obviously underage, the bar staff honoured my requests for Singapore Slings and Zombies without a twitch of surprise or disapproval. We lay on the beach, mostly, and read books and had some conversations that tried to work out just how we were going to live our lives from here on in.

It was always understood in my house that what my mother did was Work. My father had a job, and that was important – he was a teacher, an academic, and that was useful and laudable and anyway, someone has to bring in a paycheck. But the real work, the important work, the work that created a better world for everyone, belonged to my mother. She ran the house and our lives around the needs of the overriding causes that that work centred on, and we were incredibly proud just to be a part of it[14].

There were some tangible benefits. I had learned at age seven to wash my own clothes, because my mother's laundry schedule was not geared for a girl who went to school on weekdays, and I could handle a fair amount of cooking, shopping and public transportation by that point as well. My parents believed firmly that their job was to produce a fully functioning adult, no matter how inconvenient the learning process might be for them.

There, on that beach, we talked about how we needed to

---

[14]We ate no grapes from California, and once went several months without fresh milk because of nuclear testing and the risk of strontium-90. I was in my twenties before I ever tasted Welch's Grape Juice. They were War-Mongers. I was relieved to discover I had not, after all, missed out on any wondrous taste experience.

continue the work, even on the limited scale we might be capable of, and made an unspoken pact to try, somehow, to make lives that were not empty.

Periodically over the time that we spent there, my father got on that rickety boat back to Nassau for an evening. I didn't ask questions – I think he went to get massively drunk and stupid and to do a little gambling - as he always returned by suppertime the next day, with an armload of books to replace the ones we'd already devoured. On the days he was away, I would rent a bicycle and explore the island for a few hours, then collapse on my beach towel, where, after the first few times, the bartender from the hotel would, without formal request, deliver me an unending stream of those Slings and Zombies. They were pretty light on the alcohol content, but they did the trick, numbing me while I built up the callous I needed against the grief.

****

Around the middle of February, the funeral home phoned to tell us that my mother's ashes were ready for collection. There was a tiny plot in a special graveyard set aside for this, and a terse plaque with her name and her dates of birth and death inscribed on it, waiting for finality. We had, we were informed, two weeks before the flask of what was left of her life should be returned for burial.

During the last, most depressing phase of her illness, my mom had fought the increasing sadness by dreaming up some highly elaborate funeral scenarios, which she would write down and read to us when we visited.

There was the New Orleans version, where a black-draped barge was loaded with black-veiled women drinking glasses of red wine, who sang "Frankie and Johnny" accompanied by a jazz band, sailing endlessly around Lake Ontario.

There was the one my father called the "Gertrude Stein In Paris" version, where my embalmed and elegantly dressed mother was to be propped on the couch with a drink and a cigarette, hostessing one last party for everyone.

There was even a sort of "Pagan Festival" version that involved a rock band, an enormous bonfire, dancing and the destruction of every bit of property she owned.

All of them ended with cremation and scattering her ashes in some wilderness place, returning her to an earth that she had loved and cherished.

Somewhere in the turmoil of the first week after she died, someone told us that we could not, legally, scatter these ashes wherever we chose. I am not sure this was true, but we were in no condition to question it or to argue. By mutual and unspoken consent, we had resolved, obviously, to ignore this.

****

We christen ourselves "The Disposal Squad". We are a subversive organization with high, if temporary, ideals and an Oath of Loyalty to Our Cause.

It is midnight at the cottage on the lake. We have arrived hours before. One bottle of wine has been "disposed of" already.

The logistics are simple: get the rowboat out, go out to the middle of the lake, scatter the ashes.

Upon examination of the container, practice is a bit more fraught.

When we examine the "urn" it turns out that first appearances are deceptive: inside the ornamental casing there is another container, affixed with an official-looking stamped lead seal which will need to come off. This takes some innovation involving a kitchen knife heated to red-hot and slid under the seal – it takes three tries but we manage to remove it cleanly enough. We discuss the fact that we will need to put it back on again, but we are pretty sure we can reverse the process. Some wild and arcane alternate plans are devised in case we cannot.

We bundle up: it is still very cold. Ice forms at the edge of the lake and our breath puffs out little clouds of vapour in the darkness. The boathouse doors squeal in protest, we can't find the oars immediately because we have never bothered to put them away in exactly the same place every time, and in the darkness we push the rowboat into the canoe beside it, and are fairly sure there is damage involved.

Then, just as we get out into the lake and are fumbling with the business of rowing while half-frozen, we come quite close to capsizing. This causes a serious discussion of the difficulty involved in explaining – should there be anyone around to rescue us – what the hell we are doing. "The Disposal Squad" now acquires a secret handshake and theme music. We are aware that no one else on the planet but the two of us would grasp why we find this entire escapade so oddly cheerful.

And now we panic: we can't get the lid of the flask unscrewed. It maybe was soldered on, like the lead seal? We try banging it against the side, we try in turn to muscle it off with brute force. We are slightly tipsy and more than a little stoned, and this seems actually pretty funny, especially when the entire container nearly takes a dive over the edge because the top suddenly gives way unexpectedly. I fall to the bottom of the boat, giggling.

Finally, the stillness sobers us, just enough.

"She would like this," I say.

My father does not answer. He is leaning back, gazing at the stars.

When he sits up, the tears are there, but he is smiling.

"It's a good end to a good life," he says.

"Can't ask for more."

"Well, you can, Monkey-Girl. You just can't always get

it."

For the first time since I was eight and figured out that there was no such thing as "god", I find I wish there were. I understand the longing for an afterlife, a second chance, one last time to say and do the things we are too frightened of releasing into the world. I wish, for a brief moment, that I did believe, and my dad looks back at me steadily, knowing what it is I am thinking. He is thinking it, too, I guess, and in that moment, we find the strength we need, to do this one last thing for her, and the ashes float on the water, glittery in the starlight, as if they need to linger, for just a little while.

****

Back at the cottage, we open another bottle of wine. Halfway through it, a new problem occurs to us.

The urn no longer weighs as much as it should. The thought that we might wind up in jail for unlawfully disposing of my mother where she wanted to be disposed of seems idiotic. While a case could be made that "The Disposal Squad" (having now become the action wing of "The Peoples' Front For Ash Liberation") should be able to put her dust wherever we want to, that hardly seems like a fitting tribute to someone who wanted to have freedom, equality and love for an entire planet. A waste of a good arrest.

We weren't planning any graveside wailing, anyway: ashes are ashes, my father decides. Under the hearth of the cabin fireplace, there is a little trapdoor where periodically, you are supposed to pack all the ashes of fires from days gone by. We have not done this often, but my dad is pretty sure it has happened at least twice.

Somehow, we fill the container. Somehow, we get the blob of lead to stick well enough that a cursory glance does not scream "Tampered With!".

Somehow, the next morning, the first hangover of my life does not kill me.

There is a New Year's Eve party that fills every room and hallway of our house with adults and kids. There are trays of pizza cut into bite-sized squares, and chafing dishes begged and borrowed and lined up along one wall of the dining room, filled with spinach lasagne, with veal parmigiana and chicken cacciatore, with mushroom risotto, with slices of garlic bread. There are mounds of salads, pickled artichokes, black olives, fresh tomatoes and mozzarella in balsamic vinegar, and late in the night, there are flutes of champagne, trays of hazelnut wafers and bowls of Neopolitan ice cream.

There is also someone crying on the front steps in the cold, three people no one here has ever met before, locked into one of the guestrooms, two visits from the cops, and the wife of a local sportscaster naked and dancing on the coffee table in the living room.

In the morning, we survey the damage: nothing irretrievably broken if you don't count a heart or two.

Hard Rain Gonna Fall

Adam Langer was only 22 when he found himself alone in the jungle, with no very clear idea of why he was there, listening to the faint echo of voices from his platoon fading into the late afternoon, and allowed himself to do what he had not admitted to himself, even in his most secret moments, what he had been planning to do almost from the first moment he landed in Vietnam. He held his gun over his head in a universal and obvious gesture of submission and began to walk in the opposite direction of the voices.

Enthusiasm, family connections and a growing lack of sympathy for the war back home had landed him in officers' training. He had been everything the Army was looking for: bright, decently educated, personable and meticulous, and with no sense that his Commander-in-Chief was not completely correct in his declaration that this war was in service to democracy and to humanity everywhere.

Even the evidence he gleaned during training from those officers returning from 'Nam had not changed his mind, at first. He was good at getting them to talk, respectful, humble, eager to avoid mistakes, perhaps pathetically anxious to do well by "his men", whoever they might turn out to be.

And most of those he talked to did offer practical advice, which, however unpalatable or shocking it sounded, he took on board and considered, so that one could not say he was unprepared for his post. He had quickly made a friend of his sergeant, agreeing to fairly egregious re-interpretations of the orders they were given, in order to minimize the danger and exposure for them all whenever they went out from the camp. It was still dangerous, it would always be dangerous, but there were degrees of danger, and maintaining a balance between obedience and self-preservation was, it seemed, the least he could do for all of them.

His other strategy, which he had not originally believed was necessary (indeed, he had thought, at first, it was a joke, until the advice had been repeated by three other veteran officers) was to become the platoon's drug connection. It turned out to be the only way to be sure the men would have the slightest interest in his personal safety, and also ensured that even those men who did not like him had reasons not to shoot him in the back when out in the jungle.

Despite his enthusiasm, he was beginning to have doubts even before his training was complete, and these were not dispelled in any way by his experiences. While almost everyone he worked with were, at core, ordinary and decent young men, most very close in age to himself, the alien-ness of the surrounding countryside and population, the ongoing reinforcement of army-induced paranoia and the proximity of complex killing machinery created a sense of submerged and constant outrage.

There were some situations that he learned to dread. One was when some knowledge, official or by way of camp rumours, that another American had had some indignity performed on them by the Viet Cong, circulated around the base. Boredom fueled by endless routines only added to the mix. If someone that someone else knew was killed, it ratcheted up the anger. If a bomb went off in a Saigon bar, it ratcheted up the anger. If the dope ran out, it ratcheted up the anger.

He understood those times. He tried hard to lead his men to places where they would encounter no living Vietnamese, insurgent or otherwise, because no amount of reasoned argument could prevent them from taking their frustration out on people who looked exactly like the people they were supposed to be fighting. When they did meet up with some poor villager, he and the sergeant just tried to minimize the outcome to bullying and shouting and a few punches thrown, and generally, that worked.

The real danger was if they went out in conjunction with other units. Then, a spirit of competition ruled, and there was little he could do. Who could shout the loudest? Who could conduct the most violent "interrogation"? Which platoon had balls and who was faking it? If they were lucky, the villagers endured some broken bones, some theft and some vandalism. If not, the village might burn. If not, someone might be mourning a child, a parent, a lover, by nightfall.

His sergeant, recognizing that both Adam's military career and mental state were at risk, found tasks that took Adam and the few other soldiers who found these things unbearable, out away from the main action, giving them the ability to just not know anything about it. In theory, at least.

But week after week, month after month, the knowledge of not only the brutality, but the utter futility and complete hypocrisy of what they were doing wore him down. On leave one weekend, he watched as an Army chaplain harassed a group of prostitutes, who were growing increasingly angry and upset. Adam's attempt to intervene, to talk the chaplain down from his righteous fury, was met with incomprehension. His point, which was that these poor girls, most of whom were very nearly children, had no choice, and that all the chaplain was doing was preventing them from earning any money, elicited a response that of course they had a choice. They could choose Jesus. The fact that doing so would only enable them to starve to death did not seem to weigh with the chaplain. The fact that this prostitution had been forced on them by the very people espousing a love of Jesus was likewise lost on him.

At that point, all of what his country was doing to Vietnam and to themselves became clear to Adam. It would be months more, though, before his unconscious mind found its way out.

On the first day of his journey away from his past, he met no one, although he knew that certainly, he was being watched. On the second day, he entered a village. Through a combination of the sixteen Vietnamese words he knew and the five words of English one of the villagers knew, along with a number of universal hand gestures and some additional pantomime, he was persuaded to put the rifle down and eat a small bowl of rice.

On the third day, in a slightly larger village, he was met by someone who spoke rather more English. He relinquished his gun. He was asked some questions, given another bowl of rice, and he began walking again.

It went on like that for some time. Sometimes he walked, sometimes he was given rides in trucks or Jeeps. At some point, he thought there was a train, and later, a plane. He was asked questions at every stage, but at no time, he said, was it ever anything approaching an interrogation. He came to understand that he was not the first GI to do this, and that all that anyone wanted to do was to move him along, to someplace where he was no longer their problem.

After several weeks and several countries, he found himself in Sweden. He was, he was told, more or less free, and that there were people there to help him adjust to his new life. This proved to be difficult. He was, he realized a long time afterwards, in the middle of a complete nervous breakdown, and unable to understand anything more than that he had gone from one foreign and inscrutable place he didn't fit into to another place just as foreign, where only the cast of characters seemed to have changed.

Someone, somewhere, contacted a couple of sympathetic Canadian consulate staff, and he found himself, in due course, on a cold January night, standing in the front hallway of my father's house, without any real understanding of why or where he was.

****

My parents believed in a generous and open hospitality, so it was no surprise that our anti-war efforts expanded to include being a kind of informal, short-stay hostel for draft resisters easing into their new life as Canadians. Adam was our first (and only) deserter, though, and my father, after a quick visual survey, saw a boy who was at the end of his rope and hanging on by sheer nerves. He skipped the formalities of the not terribly complicated "house rules"[15] and just showed Adam the bathroom, the source of towels and so on, and his room.

We didn't, at the beginning, know anything more about Adam than the fact of his desertion. A phone call late on the previous night asked only if we could take him in, said only that it was complicated, and that he might be with us a little longer than the others. Our assumption was that he must have been at some Army base in the States and used a short leave to make his escape, and despite the constant stream of atrocities the evening news delivered to us, we had no real concept of the horrors he had been through.

Adam disappeared into the room that had been christened years before "Little Hell"[16] by my mother – it

---

[15] No hard drugs, no loud music at 3 am unless a party is already in progress, don't eat the Malomars in the fridge, and an unspoken one I only discovered years later, which was that if they hurt or upset me in any way, they would die, probably in some extremely painful fashion.

[16] A Noel Coward reference, possibly via my grandpére and his odd taste for things both theatrical and British.

was an afterthought room created when indoor plumbing had been introduced into the house, which dated to the early 1800s. It had a miniscule closet, an equally miniscule window, and was inclined, in August, to be unbearably hot.

We weren't worried that we didn't see him for the first day. He had seemed more than ordinarily tired, my father said, and we let him be. But he didn't emerge at all throughout the next day until I went up and made a forceful plea for him to come down for supper. He was quietly polite throughout the meal, helped silently to clear the table, and then allowed himself to be persuaded to leave the dishes to me and returned to his solitude.

It went on like that for days. I didn't think he had ever even turned on the lights in his room, and only rarely was there evidence that he was eating any meals he was not specifically harassed into. By then, though, we'd gotten a little more information about Adam, and we knew we were out of our depth.

We understood it couldn't go on like this. We knew Adam needed more than we had to give, but what help was needed was not clear.

"I've invited the Williamses over tomorrow," my father said.

Defeat.

The Williamses were from Georgia. Jamie Williams had served his time in Vietnam and survived it, but he had, in carefully-worded letters home, warned his mother that on no account should she allow his younger brothers to be subjected to the same fate. Mama Williams concurred: by this time she was deep into the anti-war effort and the Age of Aquarius, and she already had her plans in motion.

If there was, or had ever been a Papa Williams, I never knew, but by the time Jamie was discharged, Mama, Brian and Royal Williams were already living in Toronto.

They set up a kind of psychedelic general store catering to those hippies, teenyboppers and wannabees who needed paisley cotton shirts, hookahs, strings of beads and wide leather belts with elaborately tooled designs.

We were good friends. I hung out at the storefront, sometimes, when I needed a little space from my "ordinary" life. The Williams boys teased and flirted with me, and Mama Williams[17] was that sort of wise, earthy, gentle woman who made even the most Herculean task seem like a simple matter of just getting on with things.

"If your mother was here..."

A thousand unspoken things lay in this phrase. My mother would have known exactly what to do. She would have been able coax Adam into a place of safety. She would have known instinctively the words to unlock

---

[17] I don't know, even today, if she had ever had an actual first name.

his heart and give him peace.

The measure of our failure was staring out of the darkness: we were not equal to the task without her. It was as if her death had left us marooned on an island, tantalizingly close to the mainland, so close that we could hear the voices, even see figures in the fog of grief, yet were unable to find a way to get back.

Mostly, this wasn't apparent and we pretended that, in fact, we were all right. We were handling it. No one wants to hear the litany of woe, and what was there to tell, anyway? That we were lesser beings without her? That my mother had been our truest connection, a bridge to a greater world, and that she had made us live and feel and hold faith to the highest ideals? That without her, we were falling short of her trust in us, and that we suspected that this was not temporary; that, without her, we always would?

It was easier for me, and I knew it. I was young enough to be able to wall off my loss and my grief, storing it for some future time when I would be strong enough to confront it. My father went to bed every night beside an empty place, a visible, tangible reminder of loss. He woke to that emptiness every morning, and no amount of laughter, drugs, late night rambling, or rigorous scholarship could fill it.

But we were determined to make good on my mother's teachings. The point was, surely, to do what was needed for Adam.

And so I cooked Mushrooms Bourguignon and brown rice, and made four loaves of French bread, brushing the crust with ice water the way she had taught me. I put together a salad, and set the table, and told Adam – warned him, really – that there would be a bit of a crowd.

Jamie's wife, Barbara, had brought the baby, a six-month-old girl with enormous blue eyes and a winning collection of baby-gurgle noises and smiles, guaranteed to break the ice. They had named her "Rising Dawnchild Williams", which, to our private shame, my father and I found incredibly hilarious. We had an unspoken pact not to catch each other's eye whenever it was pronounced, because…well, really. But we were determined not to disgrace ourselves.

It was, in the main, a success. Adam was even more unforthcoming than usual with chit-chat during the meal, which we had expected. After the joints went around and the dishes were cleared, my father took the two younger Williamses out to the garage for a look at the decrepit Renault he had bought for me in anticipation of my getting a driver's license in a couple of years. Barbara, Mama Williams and I were in the kitchen clearing up, and Jamie and Adam were able to begin a conversation that was to go on for probably a year or more.

Two nights after the supper with the Williamses, Adam came into the room I used as my extended hang-out space. It had been my playroom when I was small, now it held an old TV, some cast-off comfy seating and a wall of books. My father had pointed all this out to him as a place to relax, read or just get out of "Little Hell", but we thought perhaps he hadn't quite taken it in. He stood hesitantly in the doorway, watching me roll a joint and his watching made me ham-handed, because I wasn't good at it at the best of times.

"Do you want me to...?"

I did. He handed it back to me, I lit it, and we shared it.

He looked over the bookshelves. I suggested a couple of things. He took down the copy of the Complete Works of Byron. It was an expensive edition, boxed, with leather bindings and real gold leaf edges. My mother had given it to me when I turned nine, and I knew he was going to see the inscription, that he probably had his questions, too, and I was bracing myself against them.

But he just put it carefully back into the box and into its place on the shelves, and sat down companionably next to me to watch Johnny Carson.

What I know of Adam's experiences came in snippets, from nights like these. Not about the true nature of his war experiences – he had Jamie and eventually, through the anti-war movement, other Vietnam vet friends to work out those horrors with – although the sketchy details I've written were a necessary part of our conversations. But beyond those things were other, more complicated griefs. A fourteen-year-old girl doing a balancing act of her own between public and private demons was probably not his ideal confident, but I was there, and for unknown reasons, that mattered.

Adam's guilts were legion. He was aware that for most people – for himself included – he had betrayed every value, every belief, every responsibility. That his platoon might have wound up with an officer who had no care for them. That some Vietnamese villagers might die because he was not there to rein in the white-hot anger of vengeance. That he had broken every one of what he had been raised to believe were sacred vows.

He could never go home. That was true for all of them – resisters and deserters alike – but for Adam it went far beyond the basic facts of geography and law.

He came from a strong military tradition, a family that had served for generations, and whose political stance could not possibly encompass his betrayal. They had probably been told he was MIA, that he was likely dead and rotting in some unmarked place in a foreign jungle, and that was the way it would need to remain. He could not now hurt his family more than he had already done, by shattering their belief in his patriotic sacrifice. No family member, no friend from home could ever know he was still alive or what he had done.

Most of the boys who came through our house stayed only a few weeks: long enough to find jobs and places to live, and very few of them kept in touch for more than a few months. Adam was with us for nearly a year, but that, admittedly, was due as much to our needs as to his. He was a kind of talisman for us – a symbol that, deficient as we were, we were still the people my mother had believed us to be.

We are on our way to our first ever Abortion Rights rally and running recklessly along Hazelton Avenue, Shosh trips and cuts herself on something in the street – a pebble, a bit of glass? A boy in multi-coloured patched jeans and a string of faience beads the colour of the autumn sky stops to help us. We limp around the corner to the Grab Bag where a tired girl in a halter top and a long denim skirt finds a Kleenex and a grubby band-aid and we fix Shosh up enough to survive the day. In the process, we convince our band-aid girl to come along to the rally.

The last time we see her, she is at the front of the marchers, helping to carry a massive, painted banner, and shouting slogans at the top of her lungs.

A Drum Major for the Cause (Part Two)

I met my friend Stacey in the spring of my second year of high school. I knew her to say hi to before that, as she was in a couple of my classes, but since I cut the majority of those anyway, we'd never actually talked until I ran into her at the supermarket after school one day.

By the time I was fourteen, I had pretty well taken over running the house. My father, like most men of his generation, had no clear idea of how to grocery shop and no incentive to learn. His cooking repertoire consisted of reheating spaghetti sauce, making omelets and toast, and the ability to order Chinese take-out. No one thought it strange that more complex domestic tasks, such as regular meals, laundry and vacuuming, would fall to a barely teenaged girl. No one doubted for a moment that I wasn't perfectly capable of it. It seemed expected, in fact, that I should do these things, so I just did them.[18]

So there we were, two teenage girls who merely happened to attend the same high school, pushing carts around the Produce section on a Tuesday afternoon. We were both looking at oranges or something and we did the usual awkward "Hey, I know you, you're in my Gym class" thing when Stacey's little sister stuck her tongue out, said "Who're you?" and Stacey tried to do a sort of mom thing about manners. Tracey just made faces at

---

[18]We did have help. My mother's illness had required twice-weekly housekeeping assistance, and that continued. Lest anyone mistake this: I don't think I was unduly put-upon here.

her, and we both started laughing.

It wasn't anything we said, really. It was just a feeling, a meeting of eyes over the head of an impatient kid. Something simply clicked for us. We wandered through the aisles, exchanging opinions on everything from the price of juice to shared classes to headline news. I waited for them after the checkout line and we went by unspoken mutual consent to the park across the street, found a bench near the swings so that Tracey could amuse herself and I rolled a joint.

I already knew Stacey was incredibly talented at things like drawing and it seemed she was already light years ahead of me in both skill and knowledge. Musically we shared a wider taste than most of the people we knew, we both confessed to a secret fascination with British history, and we both read a lot of poetry – Adrienne Rich, Sylvia Plath, Kenneth Patchen. She felt as alienated as I did by the skimpy nature of school – it seemed to both of us as if whole centuries were being summed up into neat little clichés that told us nothing, while the "real world" marched past the classroom windows.

In terms of politics, Stacey had insights into prejudice and patriarchy that began to instantly expand my understanding. I could almost feel my brain growing as we talked over everything that was important to us.

These are the things that are central to me, that define me despite the carefully devised protective colouring I assume. There was not much incentive to appear too intelligent, I had discovered: it irritated even pretty "progressive" people when a young girl had opinions. I had learned to express my views through artlessly sincere questions, and to listen to answers as if I was truly looking for guidance, and to smile, to joke, even when I was deathly serious. And I could see that it is much the same for Stacey, though apparently for more complicated reasons.

All this included why we are doing the family shopping at our ages. I explain, tersely, about my mom dying last year. Stacey gives me a four-sentence recap of her dad's death six years before.

"Wow," I said. "Between us, we add up to one decent orphan!"

And then I kind of freeze, because that is exactly the kind of comment that I have learned, over the years, to keep to myself. Nobody understood. No one found these remarks funny. I usually kept them locked up inside, although sometimes it meant I found myself giggling and having no way to explain it.

But Stacey – she laughed. It was a laugh to envy: rich and full and genuine.

It sealed the deal as far as I was concerned.

****

Stacey fit so well into our growing circle that it seemed like she had always been there. She was funny as well as smart, with an amazing knack for fast comeback lines that left her targets breathlessly torn between admiration and hysterical laughter. The fact that she often had to go home immediately after school to look after Tracey if their mom was working late was organized around without missing a beat, because Stacey's mother didn't seem to mind when a crowd of oddly-dressed white kids invaded her living-room and commandeered the stereo to play things like Cream or the Doors at full blast.

In almost every way, it seemed that we were the gainers: Stacey introduced us to the music of people like Muddy Waters and Howlin' Wolf, who had mostly been only names to us before. She drew endless moment-by-moment glimpses of our lives in her sketchbook with devastating honesty, and she taught all of us how to cook whole meals out of what seemed like virtually nothing at all.

As a group, we always regretted Stacey's occasionally unavoidable absence at parties; she had a gift for creating social magic. It was her idea to cover my kitchen table with shelving paper and let everyone's stoned-out artsy selves loose on it. It was Stacey who cured our munchies at 3 a.m. one night, by starting an impromptu baking session/quasi-Olympic competition, including score-cards and sports announcements. It was also Stacey (or rather, Stacey's mom) who taught us how to make instant halter tops out of cowboy bandanas.

It had become a thing in high school that my friends grouped at someone's house before school, had coffee and got stoned and then went off as a gaggle. It was usually my house, not only because it was along nearly everyone's way, but also because my dad had no problem with us getting high there.[19] For the few that lived in different neighbourhoods it was more hit-or-miss, but there were a lot of regulars gathering most week days. Sometimes, the 8 am door-pounding acted as my only alarm clock.

Mostly, we didn't do much more than pass around a joint and gulp down two inches of espresso. Some days, we also passed around someone's notes from a class we'd missed, or borrowed each other's newest favourite book, or opined on the inadequacy of our teachers.

So that's where we are. The hotknives are out, the coffee's made, and Molly is trying to find a clean mug when Adam comes in and says the phone is for me. I go out to the hall to pick it up.

When I get back, Adam is just exhaling a toke and trying to work past a couple of people back towards the door.

"That was Stacey. Tracey had a freakout about her mittens and they're running late. She said don't wait up and she'll see us at school."

Nicholas is just finishing heating up the knives on the gas element on the stove and using one to pick up the tiny scrap of tinfoil topped with a dab of hash oil and I am just leaning forward with the cardboard tube from a roll of paper towels, and Miranda says, just as I inhale,

---

[19]He had a problem with us blackening every knife in the drawer doing hash oil hot-knives, though. We argued about this a lot.

"I think it's great, the way you all are, like, *friends* with Stacey."

I am lucky. The act of holding in the smoke gives me a second or three to not say anything, but the kitchen has become suddenly quiet. Eyes are on me, and my mind is racing through a whole truckload of responses.

The thing is, I like Miranda. She is new to us; her family moved here from California last year, and we are secretly impressed by this. California has the same magical resonance as Samarkand or Ultima Thule for us. It is fabled and mysterious, the epicentre of our counter-culture dreams. At the same time, there is a kind of resentment underneath, because we are a little perplexed at how easily she has become the ultimate authority on so many subjects.

But Miranda is mostly a good sport, despite capitalizing on our respect for her assumed sophistication. She laughs when Shosh does her wickedly accurate impression of Miranda toking up and peering out from her dead-straight long hair murmuring "Oh, wow" in knowledgeable satisfaction. She seems unoffended when Andy nicknames her "The Queen of Coolth", even though it is obvious that he does not mean it in a precisely complimentary way. She has impeccably orthodox taste in music (The Dead, the Airplane, Dylan and CSNY) and her older brother deals reputable acid that isn't worrisomely cut with anything more peculiar than Nestle Quik[20].

"You know," she adds, as I am exhaling, "Inviting her along to things."

What we apparently have not known about Miranda until this moment is that she does not share the ingrained and possibly knee-jerk anti-racism that our parents have instilled into us from nearly Day One of our lives. Or perhaps it was only me who was unaware, or so heavily inoculated. This casual reduction of Stacey to the category of her skin colour shocks me utterly – I am suddenly not quite as sure of the level of shock for anyone else.

No one is looking at me now – they are busy finding other things to be doing. Well, almost no one. Adam is leaning against the doorway, arms folded, with a slightly sympathetic, slightly challenging expression that tells me there is no easy win here.

"Well," I say, and my tone is deliberately saccharine-sweet, an overflowing ladle of honey, "if I refused to be friends with everyone who is prettier and smarter and more talented than me, I'd be a very lonely girl, wouldn't I?"

There's a kind of collective exhale. Molly giggles, but Miranda turns a dark, deep scarlet.

---

[20]The Nestle Quik LSD experience was a one-off, actually, which was a pity. It was incredibly potent, easy to consume, and led to a number of in-jokes for the small group who tripped out on it the one time it was available.

Someone says "Shit! Is that the time?" and suddenly there is a mad scramble for book bags and coats and a stampede down and out into the street.

I am a little behind, because I have to back up to collect my keys from where I forgot them on the landing, and when I get outside, Shosh is waiting. The others are only a few yards ahead, but we don't rush immediately to catch up. She throws her arms around me in a bear hug. We just look at each other in a moment of – I don't know - anger? Embarrassment?

"Fucking Larry Lipschitz all over again!" Shosh says, grinning and punching her fist in the air, and suddenly we are laughing like the innocents we are, arms linked, as we skitter and slide over the icy road running down towards the subway station.

Every year, for my birthday, my father and I go out to lunch and then to a movie. The lunch is always somewhere very grown up and I get to pick, but it is always his choice for the movie. I wear my most grownup clothes, and even when I'm little, I get to have fingernail polish, and sometimes pale pink lipstick.

We eat at expensive, elegant places like Three Small Rooms or The Moorings, ordering things like escargot, oysters Rockefeller and Steak Tartare, and we see The French Connection, Sweet Charity and Goldfinger, although these entail arguments with cinema managers who are dubious about young girls seeing "adult" movies.

I turn out, therefore, to be a presentable date, when later life requires it.

Even the birds are chained to the sky...

I don't know if my father knows just how wild I am running these days, and I am fairly committed to not letting him find out.

The mutually-agreed-upon fictions are that I do not do any drugs more problematic than hash or grass, and that sexually I am as pure as the driven snow. This enables us to remain good friends, to be crazy happy when we unexpectedly turn up at the same demonstrations, to go in perfect amity to coffeehouses and concerts together, and for him to view my social life with only modest anxiety. We work out enough communication rules (mostly notes on the refrigerator door) that I no longer have a curfew, as such, as long as he knows generally where I am and who I'm with, and I phone him in the morning if I don't make it home from wherever I wound up the night before.

On the first point, he is dead wrong, and while I am aware that he worries, my defense is that he would worry more if he had any clue how undiscriminating I am about what I ingest. I try a lot of things, a whole lot of things, and what saves me, honestly, is an unexpected streak of intuition that tells me that things I don't enjoy deserve no second chances, but, more importantly, the ones I instantly like too much are things to avoid in future. So downers and heroin are off limits after the first tries, and meth, fortunately, just bores the crap out of me. No virtues here, just some twist of genetic luck.

On the second point...

I give him an expurgated version of truth, when necessary. My technical ability to avoid losing my virginity is just that: a purely technical distinction.

The trouble is that both my mother's death and my interest in boys met at the same point in time. Death and sex have become inextricably linked, and I am unable to commit to being quite that vulnerable with anyone.

We roam, as a group, throughout the city - school is something we only occasionally put any effort into. We are much too busy hanging out in Yorkville, or smoking joints in small parks around our own neighbourhood, or tripping out entire weekends away. There is always a party someplace, or a bar we can talk our way into where some band we like is playing.

One night at Stacey's, Tommy Bingham is so high on something that he spends four hours running laps from the back door, through to the side yard, around the front and in through the living room, the dining room and the kitchen to the back door again. Each time he goes by, he yells out some random number, possibly the number of laps he thinks he has completed. Stacey's mother finds him curled up asleep on the front steps at seven the next morning, when she goes out to find the cat.

There is always something going on, somewhere.

Yorkville had become the Toronto version of Haight

Ashbury or Greenwich Village, teeming with hippies from pretty much everywhere. It was colourful, crazy and fun, even after the biker gangs took notice and contrived the introduction of drugs like speed and heroin. There were clubs that brought acts in from the States – I remember standing with Ellis and his wife forever in the lineup at the Riverboat to see James Taylor, and sitting not four feet from the miniscule "stage", drinking cappuccino and smoking Players filter cigarettes. Joni Mitchell was still (barely) a "local" person, and Neil Young had rented, at some point, a room in a rooming-house a friend of mine's mother ran[21].

There is fast-talking our under-age way into places like the Colonial or Le Coq d'Or, for blues bands brought up from Chicago, and there are things like Mariposa, where you lie out in the hot sunshine and drown in folk music, and magically one summer when I am barely 15, there is Janis Joplin and Festival Express. Our little pack melds seamlessly into the larger tribe, then, and the sense of shared beliefs and drugs and expressions of our break with a repressive past hold us together.

It's just a long stream of generic party, really, all bleeding and blending into itself, long, long into the night.

There are some gatherings that have edges to them. In run-down rooms above stores selling psychedelic paraphernalia, in cheap rental-house "communes" and

---

[21]Apparently, he painted all the walls black and skipped out on the last month's rent. Disclaimer: that's hearsay, no offence, Neil.

later on, in messy "ashram" flats in Rochdale College, people we barely know share out drugs without provenance and try to sleep with thirteen-year-old girls. Eventually, it occurs to us that these parties have stopped being fun, and we go back to dealers we know and places that are less filthy.

Some nights, bands at clubs or bars we have talked our way into will invite us back to their hotel rooms. I am aware that sometimes these places aren't so safe either, but I am curiously protected. I still look much younger than other girls my age and someone always decides I am too sweet and innocent and appoints themselves my watchdog, whether I want them to or not. I am a habitual observer, though, and I see more than I should.

Sundays usually find me in a diner somewhere with friends, reliving the weekend and shoving dimes into the jukebox. There are always restaurants with bottomless cups of coffee and cheap diner food, where we talk for hours on end. One Hungarian restaurant on Bloor Street serves huge plates of dumplings with chicken gravy for a quarter, and espresso for fifteen cents, and they don't seem to mind that we take up the tables for hours without ordering terribly much.

There are, for me, meetings with groups like the Young Socialists, the Student Union for Peace Action, and the antiwar movement generally, full of university students and New Left organizers, planning protests and remaking the world.

Most of the time, the demonstrations against the war in

Vietnam run along pretty predictable lines.

We assemble at Queen's Park, have some speeches, then march to the US embassy on University Avenue, to wave placards and chant slogans. Occasionally, it is the reverse, and we start at the embassy, march to the park and have speakers, and in these cases, it's a bit more of a festive atmosphere.

It's almost always planned, legally permitted, and peaceful. We shout, we don't shove, and we try not to leave a lot of litter.

I am usually there. My father backs me up if the school calls to complain I've played hooky, assuming they catch him on a day where he isn't out supporting the cause himself. Our social lives rarely collide at home – our refrigerator notes achieve almost thesis lengths in our effort to stay in touch, and my father christens me "The Phantom Boarder" to commemorate the fact that I am rarely at home. When we do meet up, it's a dramatic event: we drop signs if we are holding them, and hug as if we had been apart for decades. People find it weird but cute.

This time he's stuck with doing the lecture scheduling for the upcoming term because everyone else has managed to be either ill, incompetent, or on holiday. We'd seen each other at breakfast and he is glad that at least one of us will be out there.

At the embassy, the crowd is really big. For some reason, although it's never been a problem before, the cops don't want the speakers to get on the steps so they can be seen. There's a little pushing and shoving, nothing much, really, and then they give way a bit, allowing us as far as the third step, and one of the guys starts leading the chants.

Near the back, I hear later, the police lines start moving in tighter, compressing people into a smaller than comfortable space. You can feel it getting a bit distressed where I am, and people start trying to hold their ground. But we're shouting urgently for the US to get out of Vietnam, to stop killing children, to stop sending young men out to die. We aren't really aware that anything is wrong.

And nothing is wrong, until suddenly and without warning, the world shifts and tilts and blurs and then explodes into a captive mob trying to run, as police start without any warning to shove people down, club them, arrest them.

We are running down the road, people are discarding signs, people are screaming in pain and anger, and I can see cops everywhere scattered among the protestors and grabbing and hitting them, until I feel a thwack at the side of my head and I go down, bouncing my knees against the pavement.

There isn't even a moment to think "This is it" or to register the panic and terror I know I should feel - a strong arm scoops me up and urges me on, half-carrying me on down the remaining way to Queen's Park, to cool shade and a motley collection of stunned, yet strangely exultant young people wandering half-dazed in the green oasis.

There is blood streaming down into one eye, and I am having a lot of trouble catching my breath, it keeps stalling on little hiccuppy sobs, and the boy who rescued me doesn't let go. He has found a few of his friends and they stay with me while one of them goes off to find some help.

A girl who is studying nursing arrives to wipe the blood up and clean the tiny cut, and encourage me with admiration for the size of the goose-egg forming on the right side of my forehead.

It occurs to me, once I've calmed down and noticed the news crews wandering among us, that I had better let someone know where I am. I insist on getting to a pay phone. My new friends – university students all – are bemused by this, but as I try to explain, it dawns on them that I am not an under-age runaway accidentally caught up in this fight, that I'm a veteran, and that, in fact, they know who my father is. We find a phone, and after assuring my dad that I'm whole and mainly undamaged, the lot of us go for coffee at their place in Rochdale College, to discuss the revolution.

I am, for this brief moment, a little hero of the cause. I am welcomed in, and invited to join up.

They are committed, the Young Socialists. They are energetic. What they are not, I discover at the first meeting I attend, is very experienced in the practical matters of organizing big things.

I try to hold back. Philosophically, they are way ahead of me. They've read up on it, studied it, and thought it all out and gotten a handle on the theoretical, and they use words like surgical instruments, taking apart the system like they are performing a really tricky open-heart procedure. It's impressive and I am impressed, and excited, electrified by new ideas, and more than a little bit intimidated.

But I am my mother's daughter, and I am struck by their inability to consider the most basic needs of a huge crowd. Little by little, question by carefully-phrased question, I start channeling my mother and the lessons learned over years of suppertime discussion: introducing the notions of things like phone-trees, march marshals, lists of speakers planned in advance so that there is a build-up towards the action and the creation of solidarity within the assembled protestors. The need to keep on topic at a demonstration, and not have it become a tasteless stew of competing interests.

After a few months, I am considered less of a cute little mascot, and more of a useful person. I am willing to do the shit-jobs: the (mostly-male) organizing teams are great on plans and short on getting the posters or handouts actually printed and distributed. Along with a few other women, I become the clerical wing of the movement. I make the lists, type up the rhetoric, buy the coffee.

And then came Wendy, like a storm wind, blowing away

the cobwebs and the competition. She objected to the way in which women's issues were shunted aside "for the greater good", she demanded that those concerns be given placement. She refused to be relegated to office work – she carved out blocks of territory to speak in, and she took no prisoners along the way.

She terrified and exhilarated us all.

One afternoon, Wendy having fought and won the right to be "last speaker" at a rally, the men had slunk off, leaving Ann and me to finish writing up the information leaflets and arranging to get them copied, Wendy invited us to ditch this thankless task and go drinking at Grossman's Tavern, where there were blues bands and a lackadaisical attitude towards ID.

"We've got to finish the leaflets."

But why should we? Wendy asks. The boys know they need to be done. It's not like paying to use the mimeograph at Hart House College is terribly difficult.

Ann points out that they won't do it.

And then Wendy voices something I have been thinking about for over six months.

"If it doesn't get done because the lazy little boys can't be bothered doing it, then they might learn to pitch in and do it next time. What are they? Babies? If they want leaflets made up for a rally they can make them themselves, instead of waiting for Mommy to do it."

She looks at Ann. Ann looks at me. I look at the copy of the leaflet text, the jar of contact cement, the drawing someone has done of a clenched fist over a peace sign, the six dollars left out to cover the costs of printing the leaflets.

And I listen, stony-faced and envious, to their giggles as they go off down the hallway to the elevators, and I try to forget the look, half contempt and half pity, that Wendy gave me as they left.

I know that she is right. I know it, but I can't act on it. And I feel like a coward, because knowing failed.

On the television, people are dying.

Not in some far-off place this time. These are students, shot down by young people close to their own age, in a square-off that brings home the gulf between two worlds.

There is the world of hope, of belief in something greater than one's self, of promises that need to be kept, and it has been pitted against the world of violence, of retaliation and vengeance, a world where death is a response to criticism, and it freezes everything it touches.

We have wept for the staggering death toll in places we have never been.

Now we weep for ourselves.

But in this shambles, I understand truly what it was that my mother had been trying to teach me. If we do not fight for others, then we, too, are at risk, from ourselves and from those who claim to be protecting us from the "other". The "other" is me. The "other" is what we all become. And only together can we survive.

The Wild Side

My first real boyfriend is an actual Irish revolutionary. At least, his father is. They are here not so much because of the "Troubles" but because the "Troubles" caused the British to start getting dangerously near to arresting him, apparently, and so they are lying low in Canada for a couple of years.

As a first boyfriend, Kenneth is a pretty good choice. He's three years ahead of me in school, and light years ahead of all of us in political experience: he's been where bombs go off. He's also extremely good-looking, he has that soft Irish accent that completely confuses my body, and he doesn't mind that I know very little about Ireland's bloody past. I think he likes telling me about it.

Meanwhile, he absolutely doesn't pressure me to have sex; instead he shows me a wide assortment of other things we can do instead, and they are more than enough entertainment for both of us.

They are, as a family, Trotskyites[22], in a very orthodox way, which is fine – I have a pretty good handle on the rhetoric by now – but they do insist that violence is inevitable, desirable even, which I disagree with. I'm careful, though, I try to object rationally, and use actual examples where non-violence has achieved good ends.

"Ah, you're soft, like all women," Kenneth's father says,

---

[22]And, curiously, still fairly devout Catholics. Don't ask me to explain this. Four decades later, it still boggles my mind.

with real affection. He likes me, all of them like me, not least because I have impeccable New Left family credentials, and because I am so sweet about my arguments.

I sturdily swallow a mouthful of Guinness, which I don't really like, but have learned to drink without flinching. It's part of the deal in being Kenneth's girlfriend. Being willing to listen, drinking Guinness, and always offering to help with the dishes even though Kenneth's mother never allows this.

****

Tommy Bingham asks me one day if I want to ditch the world for the afternoon and go for coffee, just me and him. We've done this a couple of times before – just disappearing for a few hours to some nondescript, out of the way diner down on Davenport Road, and talking about Stuff. We go shopping together, too, rummaging around in secondhand clothing places for old ballgowns and crazy forties-era hats, or wandering around Kensington Market eating bagels fresh from the bakery. It's very laid-back and purposeless hanging out and somehow it feels very natural for it to be just us.

And he just outs with it, after we've ordered coffee, just says,

"The thing is, I'm gay."

I am concentrating on stirring the sugar down into my coffee. "Yeah?"

"You knew?"

"Not knew, exactly. Felt, maybe?"

"Does it bother you?"

"Tommy, the only point where it would have bothered me would have been if I wanted to sleep with you."

He grins and assumes the Attitude of Dramatic Moment we use, body arched, head thrown back, eyes wide and one forefinger knuckled between his teeth, denoting Shock and Despair.

"You mean I'm not God's gift of gorgeous to the entire world?"

He tells me about his boyfriend, who is in university, and has a place a few blocks away. The boyfriend wants to meet me, apparently because Tommy talks about me a lot, about the wacky things I do. I juggle oranges in the grocery store, I stage fake Olympic gymnastics performances at the bus stop[23], and when I won an academic prize in history, I did a cartoony tap dance routine across the stage when they called me up. Also, the boyfriend is curious about my famous fashion sense, which consists of layering myself with gauzy skirts, neon tank tops, patterned shirts, and scarves from faraway countries till I am satisfied that any rainbow will feel shabby next to me.

---

[23]It's all about the dismount.

These are my party tricks, the way I maintain a solid place among my peers: I am the happy one, the spinny chick, the comic relief. I go along with other people's ideas, playing the Fool in other people's Tarot card layout.

Tommy's boyfriend is nice. I suspect Tommy is crazier about him than he is about Tommy, but they seem happy together. And I realize that Tommy needed to tell me about this because he is as new at having a boyfriend as I am, and that we have become each other's confidante, where we try to figure out what our boyfriends mean when they do or say incomprehensible, sometimes hurtful things.

****

One night, sitting around Kenneth's place, with the inevitable bottles of Guinness, one of Kenneth's older brothers says that he saw Tommy outside the Parkside, kissing a guy.

"Bingham's a *fag*? Boy, Peter's gonna freak!" This was from Kenneth, who was in the same grade, due to graduate that spring, with Peter Bingham.

"Unless he knows already."

"Well, he's never said."

"Would *you*? You gonna announce to the world your baby brother's a goddam fag?"

143

"Isn't he a friend of yours?" someone asks, and I squirm inside.

"I've known him all my life," I say. "Since before we started kindergarten."

"Did you know he was a fag?" Kenneth asks. I shrug. I want to say, What does it matter? How does this mean something to you? What is the problem here? But I can't find anything inside me that is not furious, or strident, or even sane.

"Is he still takin' communion, then? The little shite!" and then they are off on a rant about deviant behaviour being some kind of symptom of bourgeois decadence, and how capitalism somehow creates this.

I sit silent, wishing for invisibility, wishing for instant teleportation, wishing for silence, for courage, for a lightning strike. And I say nothing.

And I know two things absolutely: First, that it is lucky for all of us that Kenneth and his family have recently announced that they are apparently out of the woods as far as the British army is concerned and are heading back to Ireland in a few months.

And then, as well: I know, now, how a tiny piece of grit feels, when trapped inside an oyster, steadily being smothered in layers of pretty nacre till there is no grit left to be seen at all.

There is the night of the peyote.

We've read our Aldous Huxley, our Carlos Castaneda. We've read our "Bury My Heart at Wounded Knee". We think we get it, this spiritual questing, this connection to the land, this transformation of the soul.

So when things like mescaline and peyote arrive, we think we're ready to move to some higher plane, to achieve some insight into the true nature of the world. Certainly many people I know believe and speak in that hushed and holy voice about their transcendence and their revelation.

There is the night of the peyote, a night that is meant for something greater than what has gone before.

I don't really know how it is for anyone else. It isn't that way for me. It isn't that way at all.

I just got a huge grin and a giant case of happy feet, and all I did was drink, dance and party all night long.

The future's coming, and there's no place to hide

One Thursday lunchtime in July, coming out of the door at my summer job, I am absconded with by Shosh and Stacey, who have apparently been hanging around for a while waiting. Stacey has a couple of days off work and Shosh has not bothered with a summer job. Since her parents' divorce the year before, she has discovered that if she wants money, she goes around to her dad's new place and acts as if she is on the verge of tears over the breakup, and the ten dollar bills peel off like candy.

She says contemptuously that as a psychologist he shouldn't fall for it, and so he deserves to shell it out.

My summer job is not arduous: I am packing up the labs for one of the colleges. They are finally moving from a half-block of old Victorian houses into actual lab spaces newly built out in the suburbs, but since the experiments are ongoing, packing around them is slow, tricky and sporadic.

"We're going to get passports," says Shosh. She needs one, because her grandparents are retiring to live in Israel, and they want her to come visit them next year.

Stacey rolls her eyes, she thinks it's a waste of time and money, she doesn't think she will get to travel much, not until after art college, anyway. She's already been unofficially accepted, because she's brilliant and amazing, and while I'm happy for her, I'm a little bemused. I have no idea what I want to do, although it seems to be a given that university will be the next thing.

After passport applications and pictures, we slide our way into the El Mocambo. At four o'clock it's really empty, with no one on the door, and because of that, the bartender serves us cheap glasses of draft without asking for ID. It is really the surest way to do it, and especially effective if there's a band playing there that we want to see. By the time they come around to collect the cover charges, it is smoky, crowded and noisy, and the lighting's a lot dimmer, and it's too much damned trouble to hassle us.

"We should go up to the lake," says Shosh. "It's been ages."

We are all lit up like candles at the thought. Sun, water, trees, and "just us girls" - what is this but divine inspiration?

"We need groceries." I say. "And gas money. I don't get paid till next week."

I have a car. The ageing wreck of a Renault my father and I have spent innumerable weekends and evenings fixing up became mine the moment I passed my test, and while it is not pretty, it runs and is good on mileage, and has loosed me into a larger world in much the same way my first bicycle did. It also makes me pretty popular, since everyone else has to negotiate for permission to borrow parental vehicles.

It is late when we finally arrive at the lake. We have food, we have music, we have bottles of wine nicked from Shosh's mom, and we have three days before anyone will ask or care about where we are.

In the morning we make pancakes and bacon and extra strong coffee. Shosh needs it: she was into the wine while we were still on the road, and did not stop until she passed out on the couch in the main room.

As soon as the morning sun has reached the edge of the dock, we collect up towels and slide into our tiniest bikinis and are out into the light. Shosh and I slather ourselves with baby oil, in a cheerful competition on who can tan fastest and deepest, mainly to amuse Stacey.

Shosh starts griping about Molly. They quarreled back in May over something neither one of them can explain, and it's a problem. They don't hang out together unless it's a big group thing where they can avoid talking directly to each other, and this makes it difficult for me to be comfortable hanging out with either of them alone – I feel that I am being silently accused of betrayal by one or the other of them if I do.

We are worried about Shosh. She says she doesn't care about her parents' divorce, that she's fine, but she has fought with a lot of other people besides Molly, although not with as lasting effects. She is increasingly reckless about what drugs she does, and where, and with whom, and she is drinking a lot. The money thing, too, seems cynical, even for Shosh, who has always been suspicious of the world in general, and now she seems to be drifting through her days with even less purpose than I have.

Stacey and I try to change the subject, without much success, and we turn up the radio instead. I go back into the cottage and find a book – George Eliot, I think, probably "The Mill on the Floss" - and when I come out, Stacey has pulled out her sketchbook and Shosh starts drinking again and then seems to pass out once more. A kind of tired grayness seems to pervade the day, despite the brilliant sunshine, and I think that maybe this weekend might not have been such a great idea, after all.

We are saved from this creeping sense of sadness by the arrival of Nicholas and Andy, who row over from Andy's parents' cottage on the off chance that they aren't the only ones around. They roll a couple of joints and Shosh, now sociably awake, becomes suddenly the happy, funny girl we love, getting up and dancing to "Truckin'" and then wrestling Nicholas into the water and splashing everybody else in the process.

It must be teenage jungle-drums or some other random, magic charm: more people arrive, happy and amazed that any of us are here on this particular weekend. Both of the Binghams, Peter and Tommy, turn up with beer and more dope. Cathy Medvesky, who is packing up the labs with me, shows up with her sisters[24]. The dock crowds up, the music gets louder, and Peter and I are convinced into driving into town to buy hamburger meat

---

[24]The Medvesky women were legendary. They were all of them, mother and daughters, earthy, beautiful and intelligent, and so nice it was impossible not to love them.

and buns, while Stacey makes an enormous bowl of potato salad, and Andy rows back to his parents' place to scrounge packages of brownie mix, cans of baked beans and another case of beer.

When Peter and I get back, Nicholas and Shosh have disappeared, no one knows where. When they turn up again an hour later, they look suspiciously bright-eyed and self-conscious, and no one is fooled at all.

At some point, someone has found some cast-off Christmas lights in the boathouse, and used an extension cord to light them up and then string them up around the trees. There are a lot more people all the time, some whom I am fairly sure I do not know, but the mood is mellow and happy.

The party goes late and loud. We get one visit from some adult pleading in vain for quiet and another from a sort of security guy who looks after the local pier/country store/community hall across the lake, warning us not to let any underage drinking happen, which is extremely funny, since there is virtually not a single person over twenty-one there at all.

***

Three weeks later, Shosh crashes her dad's MG into the back of a Cadillac at the corner of Bloor and Sherbourne Streets, not one full minute after she picked me up for "the final cruise" on the day before he was supposed to sell it.

To be fair, it wasn't entirely her fault. Dr. Hebert didn't say "Don't drive it", and he left the keys on the hall table as he always did. He also neglected to mention that he had drained and replaced the brake fluid and might not have worked out all the air bubbles.

Shosh knew, in the last micro-second before she hit the other car, that she could neither stop nor slow down enough to avoid the crash, and braced herself against the steering wheel, the clutch, and the useless brake pedal. I, on the other hand, was merely the oblivious passenger, knowing little beyond the simultaneous sound of metal meeting metal and the slow swim towards the glass ahead of me.

Consequently, I smashed completely through the windshield face first, although it was a good few seconds before anyone noticed that I was unconscious on the rear hood of the Caddy. Due to having been completely stoned out of my skull, I had flowed serenely with the momentum, and despite the scary amount of blood and broken glass, only broke my nose.

It was a long, long time before Shosh ever trusted herself to get behind the wheel of any vehicle again, and there was finally an attempt, mostly on her mother's part, to get Shosh some counseling.

The worst thing for me was that I bled all over and completely ruined a very nice fisherman's sweater belonging to my father. Well, that and looking like a raccoon for the rest of the summer.

On Remembrance Day, a bunch of us wind up in the Brunswick House, where, like the El Mocambo and many other places, they are so used to us that they don't even bother to check for non-existent ID, but slap pitchers of lukewarm draft onto the table, collect money and ignore us. Over the last two years, they've learned that the arguments go on forever, it's just not worth the innumerable games we play, and that we always sit near the "Ladies and Escorts" door and can make a fast escape if the cops come in.

Today being what it is, the bar is filled with war veterans, and a large woman with improbably blonde hair is fronting a band playing an endless stream of musical nostalgia. The Brunswick is a "down-and-outer" kind of place where you do serious drinking, and the vets are here to do just that. We, on the other hand, are focused on our own high school social concerns, and pay almost no attention except to smile little secret mocking smiles at the naiveté of "We'll Meet Again". We've done all this before.

The first inkling we have that it isn't an ordinary day is when a full pitcher sails past my ear and smashes on the wall behind me, raining beer and glass shards everywhere.

Full scale riot.

It's like Dante's Inferno merging with Fellini's Satyricon: one-legged men are waving crutches like broadswords as men in wheelchairs charge at them with the single-minded ferocity of chair-wielding mounted knights. A blind man is hanging onto a woman in a pink sweater, flailing out at nothing and everything, the spilling beer is making the rusty carpet into a slippery swamp and the bartender is fending off an attack by brandishing a broken

152

whiskey bottle at three wrinkled warriors. The sound of glass crashing and tables overturning mingles with hoarse cries of anger, and Bleach Blonde is still gamely warbling about when the lights will go on again.

We are laughing. We crouch down and begin crawling our way along the walls toward the door. It has to be the main entrance, because the "Ladies and Escorts" door is now jammed with three ageing men in naval uniforms who are bashing the crap out of an equally decrepit man in army green. Just as we move out of the way, a couple of Army Green's comrades surge past us to the rescue, pushing the table we've just vacated out of the way and onto us, and all six of them crash, still throwing punches, into a heap of flailing bodies.

We make it into the lobby, just as a band of policemen storm through the front door, and we turn, instinctively, to our left and hurtle up a set of stairs we have only barely noticed before this, tumbling, at the top, into a quiet, serene, dimly lit and heretofore unknown jazz bar, with deep red carpet and tiny round tables, and about six people in it if you include the tired-looking waitress, a fifty-year-old Jamaican bartender and the three-piece band.

And that's where we stay, bewildered and amused, until the noise level drifting up the stairs comes down to something approximately normal, and we go down and back outside, blinking into the late afternoon sun, with crazy hep-cat jangling notes echoing in our ears and still wondering what that was all about.

Wooden Ships

Just after Christmas, I realized I was almost completely finished with high school.

Because it was when it was, most of us had wound up in what was called a "free school", run as an alternative by the Board of Education. Classes were small, interesting, and designed by the students, and, in fact, the most irresponsible links in the chain were our teachers, some of whom had to be strenuously ridden herd on to show up regularly and give reasonable feedback. Lots of things were done as independent study, and no one insisted that you had to go through any unnecessary intervening steps to get where you wanted to go.

As a result, I had worked on the things I liked so fully and so intensively that I was assessed as having amassed enough grade thirteen[25] credits with appropriately high marks that I was reasonably assured of getting into any university I chose. It had, in fact, been done without any plan or intention, and I was as surprised as anyone else.

****

My passport arrived in the mail one Friday in spring, but owing to a series of pressing social engagements, I didn't make it home until late on Sunday and only found it at breakfast on Monday morning.

---

[25] A vagary of the Ontario school system – one did five years of high school but then only three years were needed for a BA. Illogical, and out of step with the rest of the entire world.

The excitement of its official-looking stamped cover, the cover page information asserting that I was a British subject and a member of the Commonwealth (and entitled, therefore, to some unspecified services, courtesies or privileges) and the completely unflattering black and white photograph along with a list of my general physical attributes, was overpowering.

The world, as I announced to my father, was my oyster now. I could go anywhere. Europe. Bali. Easter Island.

"And who, exactly, is taking you to all these places?" he asked me.

"I can take myself," I said. "I could go to Europe for the summer."

He began to laugh. He pointed out the fact that I had never actually done anything completely alone in my life, unless I counted the time I shut my bedroom door and read the entire Lord of the Rings trilogy over a thirty-six hour marathon binge.

The fact that he was more or less accurate did not make this any easier to stomach.

I suppose I expected more from my friends, when I flourished my new acquisition in the hallway outside our Biology classroom, but the reaction was all too similar.

Molly casually voiced the opinion that since I wasn't capable of getting to the cottage and back without someone reminding me which highway exits to take, I probably could not navigate my way out of a foreign airport, let alone see anything of the rest of Europe, without a couple of tour guides and a nanny.

Shosh merely looked perplexed and then suggested I should wait until next year, when she and Nicholas had plans to backpack through Italy and Greece together.

Andy just mumbled something about "Nice idea, anyway".

I felt obscurely betrayed, but I couldn't find a single argument to counter their assumptions. It was perfectly true: I had rarely done anything completely on my own, and when I did, it was pedestrian and mundane: I went to demonstrations (where tons of my friends turned up and took charge), I shopped (but only in places I had been to a million times before), and I very occasionally drove around by myself on country roads just outside the city, looking for interesting places to sit and eat a sandwich in the sunshine.

I dawdled alone on my way home, getting off my train two stops early and meandering along Bloor Street, trying, I think, to cheer myself into a happier mood. The passport existed. I could, in fact, go places, even if this was only in theory.

Now I have to say that all of my friends, at one point or another, professed to believe in elements of some unseen, supernatural world, to things-not-dreamt-of-in-your-philosophy-Horatio viewpoints. People dabbled in witchcraft-y things, claimed to "see auras", felt bad vibes and sent out good ones. They learned to lay out Tarot cards, they followed the I Ching, they revered third-hand interpretations of Native beliefs, and they read up on Buddhism and Mother Goddess cults. I don't know how serious anyone really was about any of it. I verbally and politely adhered to these various isms and values, but I remained, in my own mind, pretty sceptical.

Still, looking up at the window of the TravelCuts Student Discount Agency, I could not shake the sudden and unavoidable impression that Fate was taking me in hand.

The poster advertised an incredibly cheap return fare to Amsterdam for students only, with a stopover in Reykjavik, courtesy of Air Icelandic. Open-ended, as long as you booked this week.

A few questions, and I was back out on the street with a hastily scribbled list of things I needed. My bank was only a block away, and it took a mere twenty minutes to convert all but a token $5 in my account into cash (for the tickets) and a thick packet of traveller's checks. Another ten minutes and I had a flight booked for Thursday afternoon, and a EurRail pass good for three months.

Dr. Lipschitz' office was another three block saunter. Since he had been my GP since I was three, he was willing to organize on this extreme short notice the shots the travel agency advised, although he seemed unwilling to believe in the necessity until I produced my passport and tickets. He did ask me what Dad thought about it, and in panicky desperation, I prevaricated and said that he hadn't seriously objected the last time we had discussed it.

When I got home, Molly was sitting on her front veranda. I said nothing, just handed her the folder from the travel agency.

"Wow", she said after a long silence. "You're really going to do this?"

My father was, for a change, at home when I finally went inside. Having decided he might have been a bit tactless that morning, he was now offering an olive branch in the form of an invitation to go out for pizza at Posilippo's.

I waited till after we'd ordered our favourite [26] , been served and had mostly demolished it before handing him my ticket, and just sat there, waiting for the axe to fall. Technically, I was still underage.

"Well," he said, eventually, "You've got some planning to do, I guess."

I should have gotten scared. There was, I think, some small, submerged part of me that was beginning to be nervous, but I was still floating on a kind of euphoric sense of this being simple, easy, a fun way to spend a few months before coming home to start university.

In the morning, I went rooting around the basement in

---

[26]Pepperoni, mushrooms, and green peppers on a paper-thin crust.

search of a backpack one of the draft resisters had left there a couple of years ago, and my old sleeping bag. I piled together the clothes I felt I could not possibly live without, added two books I hadn't read yet as well as a sketchbook, ran a load of laundry, ate a toasted bagel and then set out for school. I still owed my English teacher a final essay discussing the role of the supernatural in English Romantic poetry, and I needed to negotiate the idea that I could just mail that to him later and be done with it.

The reaction now was muted. Molly had spread the word and everyone, even most of my teachers, kept looking at me strangely, as if I had a smudge on my cheek or food stuck in my teeth. Shosh first scowled at me, then hugged me, and said no actual words. John, my English teacher, had no problems with the idea of a mailed-in essay, although he put a deadline on it, and then told me to be sure and visit Versailles if I got the chance.

At home again, I put in some time packing all those clothes and books, but when I tried lifting the backpack, I realized that even carrying it through the airport would exhaust me. I dumped everything out and began the difficult process of trying to cut down the mass of junk jewelry, hiking boots and denim everything to what I could reasonably carry.

My father watched this process without offering advice, which was probably some kind of first. Instead, he asked me how much money I had.

I had quite a lot, in my view. Every birthday and

Christmas in my life had yielded a small avalanche of five and ten dollar bills tucked into cards from faraway relatives, and my grandfather had consistently deposited fifty dollars into my savings account each September. That money was supposedly sacred in some way, and although I had occasionally raided it for emergency weed purchases or unexpected car repairs, there had still been quite a lot left.

"And university?" my dad wanted to know. I hadn't started the applications process, although if I chose to stay at home, U of T was not likely to refuse me.

"I thought about that, Dad." I hadn't, actually, but even as I spoke, a plan seemed to drop fully-formed into my mind. "I figure I can get a job in September, and apply then, and maybe work for the year."

I subtracted a long denim skirt and added a slightly grubby manila folder containing my notes for my English essay to the shrinking pile. If I wore my boots on the plane, and only brought my skimpier sandals, instead of the sneakers, that would save more weight, too. Did I need two sweaters? Probably not.

Wednesday started with Molly and Shosh banging on my door and insisting I come to school. If nothing else came from this, I thought, my reckless decision had achieved what no amount of explanation-demanding or heartfelt pleading had: they were suddenly united and it was as if the last year of acrimony had never been. It was a little bit guilt-making, though, and somewhere down with that faint nervous voice I was just beginning to hear, was the beginning of an equally faint sense of resentment.

All the way to school, and on into the hallways, they counted off the many reasons why leaving right now was just the worst thing to do. I would miss the annual end-of-year bash. I would miss the truly great summer we had all been planning. There was the Grateful Dead concert in Pennsylvania – a whole bunch of us had been planning to drive down together for that. And, really, how could I possibly enjoy all the sights and sounds of Europe alone?

Finally, luckily, providentially, Tommy appeared (the only person whose reaction had been a simple "Cool. Send me a postcard from somewhere crazy.") and dragged me away for an espresso at the Hungarian cafe while describing his latest clothing acquisition[27].

It was there that Stacey caught up with me. She said she thought I was nuts "But in a good way, honey" and then handed me a small paper bag containing a Youth Hostel membership card, a slim brochure with all the locations of their European hostels, and a hand-drawn cartoony picture of me clinging to the top of the Eiffel Tower like a pennant in a high wind and a caption that said I would probably need these and to please have a good time.

And they were the only two of my friends I actually said a proper good-bye to.

---

[27]A pair of turquoise satin trousers from Le Chateau.

****

You can tell, I am sure, even at this huge distance, that I am stalling. There is something here that is hard to come to grips with, something I still see as enormously final, and as if by setting it down in words, the trepidation will consume me, even at this late date.

****

I slept very little that night. I kept thinking of things I needed, and things I didn't need, and even after resolutely going to bed, got up several times to rethink and repack.

But if it crossed my mind that everyone else was right and I was wrong, that I could not, should not be doing this, I wasn't aware of it. I was thinking about what Iceland (where I was going to spend all of one night) might be like, and wondering if very many people in Amsterdam spoke French or English (I really had no idea, and a leaf through a world almanac and the Encyclopedia Britannica left me no wiser). I also, at 3 am, realized that I still needed to pack my toothbrush and things like that, that these would add more weight and that one of the two books would have to be sacrificed. The question of Thoreau versus Dorothy Parker sent me at last into a fitful doze.

Thursday morning seemed unreal and dreamlike.

I got up and made coffee, brushed my teeth, packed the last bits into the backpack, and went through my embroidered cotton shoulder bag several times to make sure of my passport, my tickets and my book[28]. At quarter to twelve, my father arrived back home, and we loaded my backpack into the trunk, and drove out to the airport, and ate overpriced, extremely dull airport cafeteria sandwiches. We looked at magazines at a kiosk, and my father bought me a chocolate bar "for the road".

It wasn't until we had handed over my backpack to be tagged and whisked away on a conveyor belt and began walking towards my assigned departure gate that I really noticed the fluttering in my stomach. Through a window, I caught the sight of a plane taxiing down a runway and my heart gave a funny little lurch of sudden apprehension.

There was a bit of a line at the gate.

"Well," said my dad. "I guess this is it."

I looked at him – really looked, the way you never do in the ordinary day-to-day. I think a thousand thoughts and memories were crowding and crushing at each other so hard that I might really have had no thoughts at all. A little like when you come awake suddenly out of a long and complicated dream.

The people in the line were through now, and the stewardess working at the counter was looking at us, impatiently tapping her pen against the counter-top. We went over and I checked the contents of my

---

[28]Thoreau's "Walden"

shoulderbag one more time, while she looked over my tickets and wrote something illegible on my boarding pass.

And just for a moment, I wavered.

"Dad – I think – I mean, maybe I don't have to-"

He was smiling.

"Monkey-girl, I think maybe you do." He pulled a small, hardbound notebook out of a jacket pocket. "Here. You'll want to write things down – maybe draw stuff. You'll want to remember things."

He hugged me. For a moment, I felt the rough wool of his jacket against my cheek, smelling of tobacco and of everything familiar, known and loved.

And then. as he let me go, I walked away down the corridor of the gateway bridge. At the place where it turned towards the open doors of the plane, I looked back. He was still standing there, smiling, and I waved, and went on.

###

About the Author

Morgan Smith has been a goatherd, a weaver, a bookstore owner and archaeologist, and she will drop everything to travel anywhere, on the flimsiest of pretexts. Writing is something she has been doing all her life, though, one way or another, and now she thinks she might actually have something to say.

Other titles by Morgan Smith

The Averraine Cycle:

Casting In Stone

A Spell in the Country

The Shades of Winter

The Mourning Rose

"Smith's terrific storytelling and worldbuilding will thrill fantasy fans." *(BookLife)*

Connect with Morgan Smith on

Facebook:

https://www.facebook.com/morgansmithauthor

Twitter:

https://twitter.com/morganauthor1

Check out the Blog:

https://wordpress.com/morgansmithauthor.wordpress.com

CPSIA information can be obtained
at www.ICGtesting.com
Printed in the USA
LVHW021231011222
734350LV00002B/394